The word became a kiss. . . .

Ivy's hair was hanging loose around her shoulders. Her eyes were smiling into Tristan's, the color of an emerald sea in brilliant sunlight. Before he could move away, she caught his hand. She held it in both of her hands for a moment, then lightly kissed the tips of his fingers.

Then she let go. But he held on now, twining his fingers in hers. Could she feel it, the way the lightest touch of her made his pulse race?

"Ivy," he said.

The word was like a kiss.

"Ivy."

The word became a kiss.

Don't miss the next two books
in this exciting trilogy:

Volume II: *The Power of Love*
Volume III: *Soulmates*

Available from ARCHWAY Paperbacks

KISSED BY AN ANGEL

Elizabeth Chandler

AN ARCHWAY PAPERBACK
Published by POCKET BOOKS

New York   London   Toronto   Sydney   Tokyo   Singapore

AN ARCHWAY PAPERBACK *Original*

 An Archway Paperback published by
POCKET BOOKS, a division of Simon & Schuster Inc.
1230 Avenue af the Americas, New York, NY 10020

Produced by Daniel Weiss Associates, Inc., New York

Copyright © 1995 by Daniel Weiss Associates, Inc., and Mary
        Claire Helldorfer
Cover art copyright © 1995 by Daniel Weiss Associates, Inc.

ISBN: 0-671-89145-6

First Archway Paperback printing July 1995

10 9 8 7 6 5 4 3 2

AN ARCHWAY PAPERBACK and colophon are registered trademarks of Simon & Schuster Inc.

Printed in the U.S.A.

IL 7+

For Pat and Dennis,
October 15, 1994

1

"I never knew how romantic a backseat could be," Ivy said, resting against it, smiling at Tristan. Then she looked past him at the pile of junk on the car floor. "Maybe you should pull your tie out of that old Burger King cup."

Tristan reached down and grimaced. He tossed the dripping thing into the front of the car, then sat back next to Ivy.

"Ow!" The smell of crushed flowers filled the air.

Ivy laughed out loud.

"What's so funny?" Tristan asked, pulling the smashed roses from behind him, but he was laughing, too.

"What if someone had come along and seen your father's Clergy sticker on the bumper?"

Tristan tossed the flowers into the front seat and pulled her toward him again. He traced the silk strap of her dress, then tenderly kissed her shoulder. "I'd have told them I was with an angel."

"Oh, what a line!"

"Ivy, I love you," Tristan said, his face suddenly serious.

She stared back at him, then bit her lip.

"This isn't some kind of game for me. I love you, Ivy Lyons, and one day you're going to believe me."

She put her arms around him and held him tightly. "Love *you*, Tristan Carruthers," she whispered into his neck. Ivy did believe him, and she trusted him as she trusted no one else. One day she'd have the nerve to say it, all of the words out loud. I love you, Tristan. She'd shout it out the windows. She'd string a banner straight across the school pool.

It took a few minutes to straighten themselves up. Ivy started laughing again. Tristan smiled and watched her try to tame her gold tumbleweed of hair—a useless effort. Then he started the car, urging it over the ruts and stones and onto the narrow road.

"Last glimpse of the river," he said as the road made a sharp turn away from it.

The June sun, dropping over the west ridge

of the Connecticut countryside, shafted light on the very tops of the trees, flaking them with gold. The winding road slipped into a tunnel of maples, poplars, and oaks. Ivy felt as if she were sliding under the waves with Tristan, the setting sun glittering on top, the two of them moving together through a chasm of blue, purple, and deep green. Tristan flicked on his headlights.

"You really don't have to hurry," said Ivy. "I'm not hungry anymore."

"I ruined your appetite?"

She shook her head. "I guess I'm all filled up with happiness," she said softly.

The car sped along and took a curve sharply.

"I said, we don't have to hurry."

"That's funny," Tristan murmured. "I wonder what's—" He glanced down at his feet. "This doesn't feel . . ."

"Slow down, okay? It doesn't matter if we're a little late— Oh!" Ivy pointed straight ahead. "Tristan!"

Something had plunged through the bushes and into the roadway. She hadn't seen what it was, just the flicker of motion among the deep shadows. Then the deer stopped. It turned its head, its eyes drawn to the car's bright headlights.

"Tristan!"

They were rushing toward the shining eyes.

3

"Tristan, don't you see it?"

Rushing still.

"Ivy, something's—"

"A deer!" she exclaimed.

The animal's eyes blazed. Then light came from behind it, a bright burst around its dark shape. A car was coming from the opposite direction. Trees walled them in. There was no room to veer left or right.

"Stop!" she shouted.

"I'm—"

"Stop, why don't you stop?" she pleaded. "Tristan, *stop!*"

The windshield exploded.

For days after, all Ivy could remember was the waterfall of glass.

At the sound of the gun, Ivy jumped. She hated pools, especially indoor pools. Even though she and her friends were ten feet from the edge, she felt as if she were swimming. The air itself seemed dark, a dank mist, bluish green, heavy with the smell of chlorine. Everything echoed—the gun, the shouts of the crowd, the explosion of swimmers in the water. When Ivy had first entered the domed pool area, she'd gulped for breath. She wished she were outside in the bright and windy March day.

"Tell me again," she said. "Which one is he?"

Suzanne Goldstein looked at Beth Van Dyke. Beth looked back at Suzanne. They both shook their heads, sighing.

"Well, how am I supposed to be able to tell?" Ivy asked. "They're hairless, every one of them, with shaved arms, shaved legs, and shaved chests—a team of bald guys in rubber caps and goggles. They're wearing our school colors, but for all I know, they could be a shipload of aliens."

"If those are aliens," Beth said, rapidly clicking her ballpoint pen, "I'm moving to that planet."

Suzanne took the pen away from Beth and said in a husky voice, "God, I love swim meets!"

"But you don't watch the swimmers once they're in the water," Ivy observed.

"Because she's checking out the group coming up to the blocks," Beth explained.

"Tristan is the one in the center lane," said Suzanne. "The best swimmers always race in the center lanes."

"He's our flyer," Beth added. "The best at the butterfly stroke. Best in the state, in fact."

Ivy already knew that. The swim team poster was all over school: Tristan surging up out of the water, his shoulders rushing forward at you, his powerful arms pulled back like wings.

The person in charge of publicity knew what she was doing when she selected that photo. She had produced numerous copies, which was a good thing, for the taped-up posters of Tristan were continually disappearing—into girls' lockers.

Sometime during this poster craze, Beth and Suzanne had begun to think that Tristan was interested in Ivy. Two collisions in the hall in one week was all that it took to convince Beth, an imaginative writer who had read a library of Harlequin romances.

"But, Beth, I've walked into *you* plenty of times," Ivy argued with her. "You know how I am."

"We do," Suzanne said. "Head in the clouds. Three miles above earth. Angel zone. But still, I think Beth is onto something. Remember, *he* walked into *you*."

"Maybe he's clumsy when he's outside the water. Like a frog," Ivy had added, knowing all the while there was nothing clumsy about Tristan Carruthers.

He had been pointed out to her in January, that first, snowy day when she had arrived at Stonehill High School. A cheerleader had been assigned as a guide to Ivy and was leading her through a crowded cafeteria.

"You're probably checking out the jocks," the cheerleader said.

Actually, Ivy was busy trying to figure out what the stringy green stuff was that her new school was serving to its students.

"At your school in Norwalk, the girls probably dream about football stars. But a lot of girls at Stonehill—"

Dream about *him*, Ivy thought as she followed the cheerleader's glance toward Tristan.

"Actually, I prefer a guy with a brain," Ivy told the fluffy redhead.

"But he's got a brain!" Suzanne had insisted when Ivy repeated this conversation to her a few minutes later.

Suzanne was the only girl Ivy already knew at Stonehill, and she had somehow found Ivy in the mob that day.

"I mean a brain that isn't waterlogged," Ivy added. "You know I've never been interested in jocks. I want someone I can talk to."

Suzanne blew through her lips. "You're already communicating with the angels—"

"Don't start on that," Ivy warned her.

"Angels?" Beth asked. She had been eavesdropping from the next table. "You talk to angels?"

Suzanne rolled her eyes, annoyed by this interruption, then turned back to Ivy. "You'd think that somewhere in that wingy collection of yours, you'd have at least one angel of love."

"I do."

"What kind of things do you say to them?" Beth interjected again. She opened a notepad. Her pencil was poised as if she were going to copy what Ivy said, word for word.

Suzanne pretended Beth wasn't there. "Well, if you do have an angel of love, Ivy, she's screwing up. Somebody ought to remind her of her mission."

Ivy shrugged. Not that she wasn't interested in guys, but her days were full enough—her music, her job at the shop, keeping up her grades, and helping to take care of her eight-year-old brother, Philip. It had been a bumpy couple of months for Philip, their mother, and her. She would not have made it through without the angels.

After that day in January, Beth had sought out Ivy to question her about her belief in angels and show her some of her romantic short stories. Ivy enjoyed talking to her. Beth, who was round-faced with shoulder-length frosted hair and clothes that ranged from flaky to dowdy, lived many incredibly romantic and passionate lives—in her mind.

Suzanne, with her magnificent long black mane of hair and dramatic eyebrows and cheekbones, also pursued and lived out many passions—in the classrooms and hallways, leaving the guys of Stonehill High emotionally exhausted. Beth and Suzanne had never really been friends, but late in February they became allies in the cause of getting Ivy together with Tristan.

"I heard that he is pretty smart," Beth had said at another lunch in the cafeteria.

"A total brain," Suzanne agreed. "Top of the class."

Ivy raised an eyebrow.

"Or close enough."

"Swimming is a subtle sport," Beth continued. "It looks as if all they're doing is going back and forth, but a guy like Tristan has a plan, a complex winning strategy for each race."

"Uh-huh," Ivy said.

"All we're saying is that you should come to one swim meet," Suzanne told her.

"And sit up front," Beth suggested.

"And let me dress you that day," Suzanne added. "You know I can pick out your clothes better than you."

Ivy had shaken her head, wondering then and for days after how her friends could think a guy like Tristan would be interested in her.

But when Tristan had stood up at the junior class assembly and told everyone how much the team needed them to come to the last big school meet, all the time staring right at her, it seemed she had little choice.

"If we lose this meet," Suzanne said, "it's on your head, girl."

Now, in late March, Ivy watched Tristan shake out his arms and legs. He had a perfect build for a swimmer, broad and powerful shoulders, narrow hips. The cap hid his straight brown hair, which she remembered to be shortish and thickish.

"Every inch of him hard with muscle," breathed Beth. After several clicks of her pen, which she had taken back from Suzanne, she was writing away in her notebook. "'Like glistening rock. Sinuous in the hands of the sculptor, molten in the fingers of the lover . . .'"

Ivy peered down at Beth's pad. "What is it this time," she asked, "poetry or a romance?"

"Does it make a difference?" her friend replied.

"Swimmers up!" shouted the starting official, and the competitors climbed onto their blocks.

"My, my," Suzanne murmured, "those little suits don't leave much to the imagination, do they? I wonder what Gregory would look like in one."

Ivy nudged her. "Keep your voice down. He's right over there."

"I know," Suzanne said, running her fingers through her hair.

"On your marks . . ."

Beth leaned forward for a look at Gregory Baines. "'His long, lean body, hungry and hot . . .'"

Bang!

"You always use words that begin with *h*," Suzanne said.

Beth nodded. "When you alliterate *h*, it sounds like heavy breathing. Hungry, heated, heady—"

"Are either of you bothering to watch the race?" Ivy interrupted.

"It's four hundred meters, Ivy. All Tristan does is go back and forth, back and forth."

"I see. Whatever happened to the total brain with his complex winning strategy in the subtle sport of swimming?" Ivy asked.

Beth was writing again. "'Flying like an angel, wishing his watery wings were warm arms for Ivy.' I'm really inspired today!"

"Me too," Suzanne said, her glance traveling down the line of bodies in the ready area, then skipping over the spectators to Gregory.

Ivy followed her glance, then quickly turned her attention back to the swimmers. For the last three months Suzanne had been in hot— *heated, hungry*—pursuit of Gregory Baines. Ivy wished that Suzanne would get herself stuck on somebody else, and do it soon, real soon, before the first Saturday in April.

"Who's that little brunette?" Suzanne asked. "I hate little petite types. Gregory doesn't look right with someone petite. Little face, little hands, little dainty feet."

"Big boobs," Beth said, glancing up.

"Who is she? Ever seen her before, Ivy?"

"Suzanne, you've been in this school a lot longer than—"

"You're not even looking," Suzanne interrupted.

"Because I'm watching our hero, just like I'm supposed to be doing. What does *waller* mean? Everybody shouts 'Waller!' when Tristan does a turn."

"That's his nickname," Beth replied, "because of the way he attacks the wall. He hurls himself head first into it, so he can push off fast."

"I see," Ivy said. "Sounds like a total brain to me, hurling his head against a concrete wall. How long do these meets usually last?"

"Ivy, come on," Suzanne whined, and pulled on her arm. "Look and see if you know who the little brunette is."

"Twinkie."

"You're making that up!" Suzanne said.

"It's Twinkie Hammonds," Ivy insisted. "She's a senior in my music class."

Aware of Suzanne's continuous staring,

Twinkie turned around and gave her a nasty look. Gregory noticed the expression and glanced over his shoulder at them. Ivy saw the amusement spreading over his face.

Gregory Baines had a charming smile, dark hair, and gray eyes, very cool gray eyes, Ivy thought. He was tall, but it wasn't his height that made him stand out in a crowd. It was his self-confidence. He was like an actor, like the star of a movie, who was part of it all, yet when the show was over, held himself apart from the others, believing he was better than the rest. The Baineses were the richest people in the wealthy town of Stonehill, but Ivy knew that it wasn't Gregory's money but this coolness, this aloofness, that drove Suzanne wild. Suzanne always wanted what she couldn't have.

Ivy put her arm lightly around her friend. She pointed to a hunk of a swimmer stretching out in the ready area, hoping to distract her. Then she yelled, "Waller!" as Tristan went into his last turn. "I think I'm getting into this," she said, but it appeared Suzanne's thoughts were on Gregory now. This time, Ivy feared, Suzanne was in deep.

"He's looking at us," Suzanne said excitedly. "He's coming this way."

Ivy felt herself tensing up.

"And the Chihuahua is following him."

13

Why? Ivy wondered. What could Gregory have to say to her now after almost three months of ignoring her? In January she had learned quickly that Gregory would not acknowledge her presence. And as if bound by some silent agreement, neither he nor Ivy had advertised that his father was going to marry her mother. Few people knew that he and Ivy would be living in the same house come April.

"Hi, Ivy!" Twinkie was the first to speak. She squeezed herself in next to Ivy, ignoring Suzanne and barely glancing at Beth. "I was just telling Gregory how we always sit near each other in music class."

Ivy looked at the girl with surprise. She had never really noticed where Twinkie sat.

"He said he hasn't heard you play the piano. I was telling him how terrific you are."

Ivy opened her mouth but could think of nothing to say. The last time she had played an original composition for the class, Twinkie had shown her appreciation by filing her nails.

Then Ivy felt Gregory's eyes on her. When she met his look, he winked. Ivy gestured quickly toward her friends and said, "You know Suzanne Goldstein and Beth Van Dyke?"

"Not real well," he said, smiling at each in turn.

14

Suzanne glowed. Beth focused on him with the interest of a researcher, her hand clicking away on the ballpoint.

"Guess what, Ivy? In April you won't be living far from my house. Not far at all," Twinkie said. "It will be a lot easier to study together now."

Easier?

"I can give you a ride to school. It will be a quicker drive to your house."

Quicker?

"Maybe we can get together more."

More?

"Well, Ivy," Suzanne exclaimed, batting her long, dark lashes, "you never told me that you and Twinkie were such good friends! Maybe we can all get together more. You'd like to go to Twinkie's house, wouldn't you, Beth?"

Gregory barely suppressed his smile.

"We could have a sleepover, Twinkie."

Twinkie didn't look enthused.

"We could talk about guys and vote on who's the hottest date around." Suzanne turned her gaze upon Gregory, sliding her eyes down and up him, taking in everything. He continued to look amused.

"We know some other girls, from Ivy's old school in Norwalk," Suzanne went on cheerily. She knew that Stonehill's high-class commuters to New York City would have nothing to do with blue-collar Norwalk. "They'd love to come. Then we can all be friends. Don't you think that would be fun?"

"Not really," Twinkie said, and turned her back on Suzanne.

"Nice talking to you, Ivy. See you soon, I hope. Come on, Greg, it's crowded over here." She tugged on his arm.

As Ivy turned back to the action in the pool Gregory caught her chin. With the tips of his fingers he tilted her face up toward him. He was smiling.

"Innocent Ivy," he said. "You look embarrassed. Why? It works both ways, you know. There are plenty of guys, guys I hardly know, who are suddenly talking like they're my best friends, who are counting on dropping by my house the first week of April. Why do you suppose that is?"

Ivy shrugged. "You're part of the in crowd, I guess."

"You really *are* innocent!" he exclaimed.

She wished that he would let go of her. She glanced past him to the next set of bleachers, where his friends sat. Eric Ghent and another guy were talking to Twinkie now and laughing. The ultra-cool Will O'Leary looked back at her.

Gregory withdrew his hand. He left with

just a nod at her friends, his eyes still bright with laughter. When Ivy turned back to the pool again, she saw that three rubber-capped guys in identical little swimsuits had been watching her. She had no idea which, if any, of them was Tristan.

2

"I feel like a fool," Tristan said, peeking through the diamond-shaped window in the door between the kitchen and the dining room of the college's Alumni Club. Candelabra were being lit and crystal stemware checked. In the large kitchen where he and Gary were standing, tables were laid out with polished fruit and hors d'oeuvres. Tristan had no idea what most of the hors d'oeuvres were or if they were to be served in any special way. He hoped simply that they and the champagne glasses would stay on the up side of his tray.

Gary was struggling with his cuff links. The cummerbund of his rental tuxedo kept unwrapping itself from his waist, its Velcro failing to stick. One of his shiny black shoes, a size too small, was tied with an emergency purple sneaker lace. Gary was a real friend, Tristan thought, to agree to this scheme.

"Remember, it's good money," Tristan said aloud, "and we need it for the Midwest meet."

Gary grunted. "We'll see what's left after we pay for the damages."

"All of it!" Tristan replied with confidence. How hard could it be to carry this stuff around? He and Gary were swimmers. Their natural athletic balance had given them the right to fib about their experience when they interviewed with the caterer. A piece of cake, this job.

Tristan picked up a silver tray and surveyed his reflection. "I don't just feel like a fool—I look like one."

"You *are* one," said Gary. "And I want you to know I'm not that much of a fool to believe your line about earning money for the Midwest meet."

"What do you mean?"

Gary snatched up a spaghetti mop and held it so its spongy strings flopped over his head. "Oh, Tristy," he said in a high-pitched voice, "what a surprise to see you at my mother's wedding!"

"Shut up, Gary."

"Oh, Tristy, put down that tray and dance

with me." Gary smiled and patted the mop's spongy head.

"Her hair doesn't look like that."

"Oh, Tristy, I just caught my mother's bouquet. Let's run away and get married."

"I don't want to marry her! I just want her to know I exist. I just want to go out with her. Once! If she doesn't like me, well . . ." Tristan shrugged as if it didn't matter, as if the worst crush he'd ever had in his life might really disappear overnight.

"Oh, Tristy—"

"I'm going to kick your—"

The kitchen door swung open. "Gentlemen," said Monsieur Pompideau, "the wedding guests have arrived and are ready to be served. Could Fortune be so smiling upon us that you two *experienced* garçons would be available to help serve them?"

"Is he being sarcastic?" Gary asked.

Tristan rolled his eyes, and they hurried to join the other waiters at their stations.

For the first ten minutes, Tristan occupied himself with watching the other workers, trying to learn his job. He knew that girls and women liked his smile, and he used it for all it was worth, especially when the caviar he was serving leaped like a fully evolved fish into an older woman's lap.

He worked his way around the large reception hall, searching for Ivy, sneaking peeks while big-bellied men unloaded his trays. Two of them went away wearing their drinks and muttering, but he barely noticed. All he could think about was Ivy. If he came face-to-face with her, what would he say? "Have some crab balls?" Or perhaps, "May I suggest *le ballée de crabbe?*"

Yeah, that would impress her.

What kind of guy had he turned into? Why should he, Tristan Carruthers, a guy hanging up in a hundred girls' lockers (maybe a slight exaggeration) need to impress her, a girl uninterested in hanging in his locker or anybody else's, for all he could tell? She walked the same halls he did, but it was as if she traveled in another world.

He'd noticed her on her first day at Stonehill. It wasn't just her different kind of beauty, that wild tangle of kinky gold hair and her sea green eyes, that made him want to look and look, and touch. It was the way she seemed free of things other people were caught up in— the way she focused on the person she was talking to, without scanning the crowd to see who else was there; the way she dressed not to look like everyone else; the way she lost herself in a song. He had stood in the doorway of the school music room one day, mesmerized. Of course, she hadn't even noticed him.

He doubted that Ivy knew he existed. But was this catering thing really a good way to clue her in? After recovering a fat crab ball that had rolled to a stop between some pointy-toed shoes, he was starting to doubt it.

Then he saw her. She was in pink—and pink and pink: yards of pink sparkly stuff that fell off her shoulders and must have had some kind of hoop under its skirt.

Gary passed by him then. Tristan turned a little too quickly and their elbows hit. Eight glasses shivered on their stems, spilling dark wine.

"Some dress!" Gary said with a quiet snicker.

Tristan shrugged. He knew the dress was cheesy, but he didn't care. "Eventually she'll take it off," he reasoned.

"Pretty cocky there, buddy."

"That's not what I meant! What I—"

"Pompideau," Gary warned, and the two of them quickly parted. The caterer snagged Tristan, however, and hauled him into the kitchen. When Tristan emerged again, he was carrying a low-lying spread of vegetables and a shallow bowl of dip—stuff that couldn't spill. He noticed that some of the guests seemed to recognize him now and moved quickly out of his way when he approached. Which meant he carried a full tray round and round, hardly needing to look where he was going, and had plenty of time to scope out the party.

"Hey, swimmer. Sssswimmer."

It was someone from school calling him, probably one of Gregory's friends. Tristan had never liked the guys or girls in Gregory's crowd. All of them had money and flaunted it. They did some stupid things and were always looking for a new thrill.

"Sssswimmer, are you deaf?" the guy called out. Eric Ghent, thin-faced and blond, lounged against the wall, one hand hanging on to a candle sconce.

"I'm sorry," said Tristan. "Were you talking to me?"

"I know you, Waller. I know you. Is this what you do between laps?" Eric let go of the sconce and swayed a little.

"This is what I do so I can afford to do laps," Tristan replied.

"Great. I'll buy you ssssome more laps."

"What?"

"I'll make it worth your time, Waller, to get me a drink."

Tristan looked Eric over. "I think you've already had one."

Eric held up four fingers, then dropped his hand limply.

"Four," Tristan corrected himself.

"This is a private party," Eric said. "They'll serve under age. Private party or not, they'll serve whatever to whoever old Baines wants them to ssserve. The man buys everybody, you know."

That's where Gregory learned it from, Tristan thought to himself. "Well, then," he said aloud, "the bar's over there." He tried to move on, but Eric placed himself squarely in front of Tristan. "Problem is, I've been cut off."

Tristan took a deep breath.

"I need a drink, Waller. And you need some bucks."

"I don't take tips," Tristan said.

Eric started to laugh. "Well, maybe you don't *get* them—I've been watching you bump around. But I think you'd take 'em."

"Sorry."

"We need each other," Eric said. "We've got a choice. We can help each other or hurt each other."

Tristan didn't reply.

"Know what I mean, Waller?"

"I know what you mean, but I can't help you out."

Eric took a step toward him. Tristan took a step back. Eric stepped closer again.

Tristan tensed. Gregory's friend was a lightweight in Tristan's book, the same height but nowhere near as broad as Tristan. Still, the guy was drunk and had nothing to lose—such as a large tray loaded with vegetables.

No problem, thought Tristan. A quick sidestep would send Eric plunging to his knees, then flat on his face.

But Tristan hadn't counted on the bridal party passing through at that moment. Catching sight of them out of the corner of his eye, he suddenly had to shift direction. He slammed into the lurching Eric. Celery and cauliflower, mushrooms and pepper curls, broccoli and snow peas were launched toward a chandelier, then rained down upon the party.

And then she looked at him. Ivy, sparkling Ivy. For a moment their eyes met, hers round as the cherry tomatoes that rolled onto her mother's train.

Tristan was sure that she finally knew he existed.

And he was just as sure that she'd never go out with him. Never.

"Maybe you were right, Ivy," Suzanne whispered as they looked down at the splatter of raw vegetables. "On land, Tristan's a klutz."

What is he doing here? Ivy wondered. Why didn't he stay in his pool, where he belongs? She knew her friends would be convinced he was following her around, and it embarrassed her.

Beth picked her way toward them, spearing a tomato with her high heel. "Perhaps this is how he earns money," she said, reading Ivy's troubled face.

Suzanne shook her head. "Throwing broccoli at the bride?"

"That cute redheaded swimmer is here, too," Beth went on. Her frosted hair was up on her head that night, making her look even more like a sweet-faced owl.

"Neither of them knows what he's doing," Suzanne observed. "They're here just for tonight." Ivy sighed.

"I guess Tristan's hard up," Beth said.

"For money or for Ivy?" Suzanne asked, and they both laughed.

"Oh, come on, Ivy," Beth said, touching her gently on the arm. "It's funny! I bet his eyes got big when he saw what you were wearing."

Suzanne made her eyes gigantic and started humming the theme from *Gone with the Wind*.

Ivy grimaced. She knew she looked like Scarlett O'Hara dropped in a bucket of glitter.

But it was the gown her mother had picked out especially for her.

Suzanne kept humming.

"I bet Gregory's eyes got big when he saw what you *weren't* wearing," Ivy told her friend, hoping to shut her up. Suzanne was in a plunging black sheath.

"I certainly hope so!"

"And speaking of," said Beth.

"There you are, Ivy." Gregory's voice was warm and almost intimate. Suzanne swung toward him. He offered Ivy his arm. "We're expected at the head table."

With her hand resting lightly on his arm, Ivy fell into step beside him, wishing Suzanne could go in her place. Her mother looked up as the two of them approached, beaming at Ivy in her plantation-poof gown.

"Thank you," Ivy said as Gregory held out her chair for her.

He smiled at her—that secret kind of smile she had first seen at the swim meet. He leaned down, his lips close to her bare neck. "My pleasure, ma'am."

Ivy's skin prickled a little. He's playing, she told herself. Just play along. Since the swim meet, he had been teasing her and trying to be friendly, and she knew she should give him credit for that; but Ivy preferred the old, cold Gregory.

She had understood completely his icy response when she arrived at his school. She knew it must have been a terrible shock when he found out that Maggie was moving her brood from their apartment in Norwalk to one his father was leasing in Stonehill, and that this was in preparation for marriage.

Andrew and Maggie's affair had begun years earlier. But affairs were affairs, people said, and Andrew and her mother were such an odd romantic pair—a very wealthy and distinguished president of a college and his wife's hairdresser. Who'd have guessed that years after their fling, years after Andrew's divorce, he and Maggie would tie the knot?

It had been a shock even to Ivy. Her own father had died when she was an infant. She had grown up watching her mother run through a series of boyfriends, and thought it would always be that way.

Ivy leaned forward to look down the table at her mother. Andrew caught her eye and smiled, then nudged his new wife. Maggie beamed back at Ivy. She looked so happy.

Angel of love, Ivy prayed silently, watch over Mom. Watch over all of us. Make us a loving family, loving and strong.

"Should I tell you that your—uh—sparkles are dipping in the soup?"

Ivy sat back quickly. Gregory laughed and offered her his napkin.

"That dress can get you in a lot of trouble," he teased. "It nearly blinded Tristan Carruthers."

Ivy could feel the warmth spreading in her cheeks. She wanted to point out that it was Eric, not she—

"I feel sorry for the table he's waiting on tonight. He and that other jock," Gregory said, still grinning. "I hope it's not ours."

They both glanced around the room.

Me too, Ivy thought, me too.

Shortly after the raw vegetable shower, Tristan was told he could leave and should leave, immediately. Tired and humiliated, he would have been glad to clear out, but he was Gary's ride home. So he poked around behind the kitchen until he found a storeroom to hole up in.

It was dark and peaceful there, its shelves stacked with large boxes and cans. Tristan had just settled down comfortably on a carton when he heard rustling behind him. Mice, he thought, or rats. He really didn't care. He tried to console himself, imagining himself standing on the top winner's block, the flag of the United States rising behind him while the anthem played, Ivy watching on TV and sorry she had missed her chance to go out with him.

"I'm an idiot!" he said, dropping his head in his hands. "I could have any girl I want and—"

A hand rested lightly on his shoulder.

Tristan's head shot up and he looked into the pale, triangular face of a kid. The kid, who looked about eight years old, was all dressed up, his tie knotted tightly and his dark hair plastered down. He must have been one of the wedding guests.

"What are you doing in here?" Tristan demanded.

"Would you get me some food?" the boy asked.

Tristan frowned, annoyed that he had to share his hideout, a cozy place for pining over Ivy. "Why can't you get your own food?"

"They'll see me," said the boy.

"Well, they'll see me too!"

The boy's mouth formed a thin, straight line. His jaw was set. But his eyes looked uncertain and his brow was puckered.

Tristan spoke in a gentler voice. "Looks as if you and I are up to the same thing. Hiding out."

"I'm really hungry. I didn't eat breakfast or lunch," the kid said.

Through the door, which was open a crack, Tristan could see the other waiters whisking in and out. They had just begun to serve the dinner.

"I might have something in my pocket," he told the kid, and pulled out a squashed crab ball, several shrimp, three stalks of stuffed celery, a handful of cashews, and something unidentifiable.

"Is that sushi?" asked the boy.

"Got me. All of this was on the floor and then it was in my pocket, and I don't know where this jacket has been, it was rented."

The boy nodded solemnly and studied Tristan's selection. "I like shrimp," he said at last, picking up one, spitting on it, then wiping it clean with his finger. He did this with each shrimp in turn, then the crab ball, then the celery. Tristan wondered if he'd spit on each tiny nut. He wondered how big a problem this kid was carrying around to make him not eat all day and hide in a dark storeroom.

"So," said Tristan, "I guess you don't really like weddings."

The kid glanced at him, then took a nibble out of the unrecognizable thing.

"Do you have a name, kid?"

"Yes."

"Mine's Tristan. What's yours?"

The kid set aside the unrecognizable hors d'oeuvre and began working on the nuts. "I'd like dinner," he said. "I'm real hungry."

Tristan peered through the crack. Waiters were rushing in and out of the kitchen. "Too many people around," he said.

"Are you in some kind of trouble?" the kid asked.

"Some kind. Nothing serious. How about you?"

"Not yet," said the kid.

"But you will be?"

"When they find me."

Tristan nodded. "I guess you've already figured out that you can't stay here forever."

Squinting, the boy surveyed the shelves in the dim room, as if he were seriously considering its possibilities.

Tristan laid his hand gently on the boy's arm. "What's the problem, pal? Want to tell me about it?"

"I'd really like dinner," the boy said.

"All right, all right!" Tristan said irritably.

"I'd like dessert, too."

"You'll take what I can get!" snapped Tristan.

"Okay," the boy replied meekly.

Tristan sighed. "Don't mind me. I'm grouchy."

"I don't mind you," the boy assured him softly.

"Look, pal," Tristan said. "Only one waiter left, and plenty of food. You coming with me? Good! There he goes. Raiders, take your mark, get set—"

"Where's Philip?" Ivy asked.

The wedding party was halfway through their dinner when she realized that her brother wasn't in his chair. "Have you seen Philip?" she said, rising from her seat.

Gregory pulled her back down. "I wouldn't worry, Ivy. He's probably messing around somewhere."

"But he hasn't eaten all day," said Ivy.

"Then he's in the kitchen," Gregory said simply.

Gregory didn't understand. Her little brother had been threatening to run away for weeks. She had tried to explain to Philip what was happening and how nice it would be in their big house with a tennis court and a view of the river, and how great it would be to have Gregory as an older brother. He didn't buy any of it. Actually, Ivy didn't, either.

She pushed back her chair, too quickly for Gregory to stop her, and hurried off to the kitchen.

"Dig in," said Tristan. On the box between the kid and him sat a mound of food—charred filet mignon, shrimp, an assortment of vegetables, salad, and rolls with lots of whipped butter.

"This is pretty good," said the kid.

"Pretty good? This is a feast!" said Tristan. "Eat up! We'll need our strength to capture dessert."

He saw a trace of a smile, then it disappeared.

"Who're you in trouble with?" the boy wanted to know.

Tristan chewed for a moment. "It's the caterer, Monsieur Pompideau. I was working for him and spilled some things. You know, I wet a few people's pants."

The boy smiled, a bigger smile this time. "Did you get Mr. Lever?"

"Should I have aimed for him?" Tristan asked.

The kid nodded, his face brightened considerably by this thought.

"Anyway, Pompideau told me to stick to things that didn't spill. Imagine that."

"You know what I'd tell *him*?" said the kid. The pucker in his brow was gone. He was gulping down food and talking with his mouth full. He looked about a hundred times better than he had fifteen minutes earlier.

"What?"

"I'd tell him: Stick it in your ear!"

"Good idea!" said Tristan. He picked up a piece of celery. "Stick it in your ear, Pompideau."

The kid laughed out loud, and Tristan wedged in the stalk.

"Stick it in your other ear, Pompideau!" the kid commanded.

Tristan snatched up another piece of celery.

"Stick it in your hair, Dippity-doo!" the boy crowed, carried away with the game.

Tristan took a handful of shredded salad and dropped it on his head. Too late he realized the greens were covered with vinaigrette.

The kid threw back his head and laughed. "Stick it in your nose, Doo-be-doo!"

Well, why not? Tristan thought. He had been eight years old once, and remembered how funny noses and boogers seemed to little boys. He found two shrimp tails and stuck them in, their pink fins flaring out of his nostrils.

The kid was falling off his box laughing. "Stick it in your teeth, Doo-be-doo!"

Two black olives worked well, each stuck on a tooth, so he had two black incisors.

"Stick it in—"

Tristan was busy adjusting his celery and shrimp tails. He hadn't noticed how the crack of light had widened. He didn't see the kid's face change. "Stick it where, Doo-be-doo?"

Then Tristan looked up.

3

Ivy froze. She was stunned by the sight of Tristan, celery stuck in his ears, salad shreds in his hair, something squishy and black on his teeth, and—hard as it was to believe that someone older than eight would do this—shrimp tails sticking out of his nose.

Tristan looked just as stunned to see her.

"Am I in trouble?" Philip asked.

"I think I am," Tristan said softly.

"You're supposed to be in the dining room, eating with us," Ivy told Philip.

"We're eating in here. We're having a feast."

She looked at the assortment of food piled on the plates between them, and one side of her mouth curled up.

"Please, Ivy, Mom said we could bring any friends we wanted to the wedding."

"And you told her you didn't have any, remember? You said you didn't have one friend in Stonehill."

"I do now."

Ivy looked at Tristan. He was careful to keep his eyes down, concentrating on the celery, shrimp, and squashed black olives, lining them up on the box in front of him. Disgusting.

"Mademoiselle!"

"It's Doo-be-doo!" cried Philip. "Close the door! Please, Ivy!"

Against her better judgment, she did, for strange as it seemed, her brother looked happier than he had in weeks. With her back to the storeroom, Ivy faced the caterer.

"Is something wrong, mademoiselle?"

"No, sir."

"Are you *très certaine?*"

"*Très,*" she replied, taking Monsieur Pompideau's arm and walking him away from the door.

"Well, you are wanted in the dining room," he said crisply. "It is time for the toast. Everyone is waiting."

Ivy hurried out. They were indeed waiting, and she couldn't avoid an entrance. Ivy blushed as she crossed the room. Gregory pulled her toward him, laughing. Then he handed her a champagne glass.

A friend of Andrew's made the toast. It went on and on.

"Hear, hear," all the guests cried out at last.

"Hear, hear, sister!" Gregory said, and drank down the contents of the glass. He held it out to be filled again.

Ivy took a small sip from hers.

"Here, here, sister," he said again, but low and soft this time, his eyes burning with a strange light. He clinked his glass against hers and downed the champagne once more.

Then he pulled Ivy to him, so close she couldn't breathe, and kissed her hard on the mouth.

Ivy sat at her piano, staring at the same measures of music she had opened to five minutes before, one hand resting lightly on her lips. She dropped her hand down to the yellowed keys and ran her fingers over them, eliciting ripples of music, not quite in tune. Then she ran her tongue over her lips. They weren't really bruised; it was all in her mind.

Still, she was glad that she had talked her mother into letting Philip and her stay in their apartment until after the honeymoon. Six days alone with Gregory in that huge house on the ridge was more than she could face, especially with Philip acting up.

Philip, who in their crowded Norwalk apartment had rigged up old curtains around his bed because he wanted to be away from "the girls," had been begging to sleep with her for the past two weeks. The night before the wedding she had let him bring his sleeping bag into her room. She had awakened to find him and Ella the cat on top of her. After their long day at the wedding, she'd probably let him sleep in her room again that night.

He was on the floor behind her, playing with his baseball cards, arranging dream teams on the scatter rug. As usual, Ella wanted to stretch out in the middle of the baseball diamond. The pitcher rode on her black belly, up and down. Every once in a while, a soft phrase would escape Philip. "Fly ball deep to center field," he'd whisper, then Don Mattingly would make his home-run trot around the bases.

I shouldn't let him stay up this late, Ivy thought. But she herself couldn't sleep, and she was glad for his company. Besides, Philip had eaten such a conglomeration of party food, and so many sweets on top of that—thanks to Tristan—he'd probably throw up all over his sleeping bag. And clean sheets, like most everything else in their apartment, were packed.

"Ivy, I decided," Philip said suddenly. "I'm not going to move."

"What?" She lifted her legs and spun around on the piano bench.

"I'm staying here. Do you and Ella want to stay with me?"

"And what about Mom?"

"She can be Gregory's mother now," Philip said.

Ivy winced, the way she did each time her mother made a fuss over Gregory. Maggie was warmhearted and affectionate—and trying hard, much too hard. She had no idea how ridiculous Gregory found her.

"Mom will always be *our* mother, and right now she needs us."

"Okay," Philip said agreeably. "You and Ella go. I'm going to ask Tristan to move in with me."

"Tristan!"

He nodded, then said softly to himself, "Walked the batter. Tying run coming up to the plate."

Apparently he had made up his eight-year-old mind and didn't figure that the matter needed to be discussed further. He played contentedly. It was the strangest thing, how he had begun to play again after his fun with Tristan.

What had Tristan said to Philip that helped him so? Perhaps nothing, Ivy thought. Perhaps instead of trying to explain their mother's marriage for the last three weeks, she should have just stuck some shrimp in her nose.

"Philip," she said sharply.

The tying run had to come home before he was willing to talk to her again. "Huh?"

"Did Tristan say anything to you about me?"

"About you?" He thought for a moment. "No."

"Oh." Not that I care, she told herself.

"Do you know him?" Philip asked.

"No. No, I just thought that maybe, after I found you in the storeroom, he'd say something about me."

Philip's brow knitted. "Oh, yeah. He asked me if you like to wear pink dresses like that, and if you really believe in angels. I told him about your collection of statues."

"What did you tell him about my dress?"

"Yes."

"Yes?" she exclaimed.

"You told Mommy you thought it was pretty."

And her mother had believed her. Why shouldn't Philip?

"Did Tristan say why he was working there tonight?"

"Yup."

The inning was over. Philip was setting up a new defense.

"Well, why?" Ivy asked, exasperated.

"He has to make some money for a swim

meet. He's a swimmer, Ivy. He goes to other states and swims. He needs to fly, I can't remember where."

Ivy nodded. Of course. Tristan was just hard up, earning his way. She should stop listening to Suzanne.

Philip stood up suddenly. "Ivy, don't make me go to that big house. Don't make me go. I don't want to eat dinner with him!"

Ivy reached out for her brother. "New things always seem scary," she reassured him. "But Andrew has been nice to you, right from the start. Remember who bought you Don Mattingly's rookie card?"

"I don't want to eat dinner with Gregory."

She didn't know what to say to that.

Philip stood next to her, his fingers moving silently over the old piano's keys. When he'd been younger he used to do that and sing the tunes he was supposed to be playing.

"I need a hug," she said. "How about it?"

He gave her an unenthusiastic one.

"Let's do our new duet, okay?"

He shrugged. He'd play along with her, but the happiness that she had glimpsed in him earlier had disappeared.

They were five measures through when he slammed his hands down on the piano. He banged and banged and banged.

"I won't go! I won't go! I won't!"

Philip burst into tears, and Ivy pulled him toward her, letting him sob in her arms. When he had settled into exhausted hiccups, she said, "You're tired, Philip. You're just tired," but she knew it was more than that.

While he rested against her she played for him his favorite songs, then softened the medley into lullabies. Soon he was almost asleep and much too big for her to carry into bed.

"Come on," she said, helping him up from the bench. Ella followed them into her room.

"Ivy."

"Hmmm?"

"Can I have one of your angels tonight?"

"Sure. Which one?"

"Tony."

Tony was the dark brown one, carved out of wood, Ivy's father angel. She stood Tony next to the sleeping bag and Don Mattingly. Then Philip crawled into the bag, and she zipped him in.

"Do you want to say an angel prayer?" she asked.

Together they said, "Angel of light, angel above, take care of me tonight. Take care of everyone I love."

"That's you, Ivy," Philip added, and closed his eyes.

4

Ivy felt as if she floated through most of the week that followed the wedding, with one day slipping into the next, marked only by frustrating discussions with Philip. Suzanne and Beth teased her about her absent-mindedness, but more gently than usual. Gregory passed her in the hall once or twice and made little jokes about straightening up his room before Friday. Tristan didn't cross her path that week—at least she didn't see him.

Everyone in school knew by then about her mother and Andrew's marriage. The wedding had made all the local papers as well as the *New York Times.* Ivy shouldn't have been surprised, for Andrew was often in the paper, but it was odd to see photos of her mother as well.

Friday morning finally arrived, and Ivy nosed her rusty little Dodge out of the apartment driveway, feeling suddenly homesick for every crowded, noisy, dilapidated rental place her family had ever lived in. When she returned from school that afternoon, she'd enter a different driveway, one that climbed a ridge high above the train station and river. The road to the house hugged a low stone wall and ran between patches of woods, daffodils, and laurel. Andrew's woods, daffodils, and laurel.

That afternoon Ivy picked up Philip from school. He had given up the fight and rode next to her in silence. Halfway up the ridge, Ivy heard a motorcycle on the bend above them, roaring downhill. Suddenly the cyclist and she were face-to-face. She was already as far to the right as she could get. Still he came head-on. Ivy slammed on her brakes. The cycle swerved dangerously close to them, then sped past.

Philip's head spun around, but he didn't say anything. Ivy glanced in the rearview mirror. It was probably Eric Ghent. She hoped Gregory was with him.

But Gregory was waiting for them at the house, along with Andrew and her mother, who were just back from their honeymoon. Her mother greeted them with big hugs and lipstick kisses and a cloud of some new kind of perfume. Andrew took both of Ivy's hands in his. He was wise enough to smile at but not touch Philip. Then Ivy and Philip were turned over to Gregory.

"I'm the tour guide," he said. Leaning toward Philip, he warned, "Stay close. Some of these rooms are haunted."

Philip looked around quickly, then glanced up at Ivy.

"He's just kidding."

"I'm not," said Gregory. "Some very unhappy people have lived here."

Philip glanced up at Ivy again. She shook her head.

On the outside the house was a stately white clapboard home with heavy black shutters. Wings had been added to each side of the main structure. Ivy would have liked to live in one of the smaller wings with their deep sloping roofs and dormer windows.

In the main part of the house, some of the high-ceilinged rooms seemed as large as apartments that they had once lived in. The house's wide center hall and sweeping stair separated the living room, library, and solarium from the dining room, kitchen, and family room. Beyond the family room was a gallery leading to the west wing with Andrew's office.

Since her mother and Andrew were talking

in the office, the downstairs tour stopped at the gallery, in front of three portraits: Adam Baines, the one who had invested in all the mines, looking stern in his World War I uniform; Judge Andy Baines, in his judicial robes; and Andrew, dressed in his colorful academic gown. Next to Andrew there was a blank spot on the wall.

"Makes you wonder who's going to hang there," Gregory remarked dryly. He smiled, but his gray, hooded eyes had a haunted look. For a moment Ivy felt sorry for him. As Andrew's only son, he must have felt a lot of pressure to do well.

"You will," she said softly.

Gregory looked in her eyes, then laughed. His laughter was touched with bitterness.

"Come upstairs," he said, taking her hand and leading her to the back stairway that ran up to his room. Philip tagged along silently.

Gregory's room was large and had only one thing in common with other guys' rooms—an archaeological layer of discarded underwear and socks. Beneath that, it showed money and taste: dark leather chairs and glass tables, a desk and computer, and a large entertainment center. Covering the walls were museum prints with striking geometric shapes. In the center of it all was a king-size waterbed.

"Try it," Gregory urged.

Ivy leaned down and jiggled it tentatively with her hand.

He laughed at her. "What are you afraid of? Come on, Phil"—no one calls him Phil, Ivy thought—"show your sister how. Climb on top and give it a good roll around."

"I don't want to," said Philip.

"Sure you do." Gregory was smiling, but his tone of voice threatened.

"Nope," said Philip.

"It's a lot of fun." Gregory grasped Philip's shoulders and pushed him back forcefully toward the bed.

Philip resisted, then tripped and fell onto it. He sprang off just as quickly. "I hate it!" he cried.

Gregory's mouth hardened into a line.

Ivy then sat down on the bed. "It *is* fun," she said. She bounced slowly up and down. "Try it with me, Philip." But he had moved out into the hallway.

"Lie back on it, Ivy," Gregory urged her, his voice low and silky.

When she did, he lay down close to her.

"We really should get to our unpacking," Ivy said, sitting up quickly.

They crossed through a low-roofed passage that was just above the gallery and into the section of the main house where Philip and she had their bedrooms.

Her door was closed and when she opened it, Philip rushed through to Ella, who was stretched out luxuriously on Ivy's bed. Oh no, Ivy groaned silently as she glanced around the elaborately decorated room. She had feared the worst when her mother said she was in for a big surprise. What she saw was lots of lace, white wood trimmed with gold, and a canopy bed. "Princess furniture," she muttered aloud.

Gregory grinned.

"At least Ella looks at home. She's always thought of herself as a queen. Do you like cats, Gregory?"

"Sure," he said, sitting on the bed next to Ella. Ella promptly got up and walked to the other end of the bed.

Gregory looked annoyed.

"That's a queen for you," Ivy said lightly. "Well, thanks for the tour. I've got a lot to unpack."

But Gregory lounged back on her bed. "This was my room when I was a kid."

"Oh?"

Ivy lifted an armload of clothes from a garment bag and pulled open a door to what she thought was a closet. Instead she faced a set of steps.

"That was my secret stairway," Gregory said.

Ivy peered up into the darkness.

"I used to hide up in the attic when my mother and father fought. Which was every day," Gregory added. "Did you ever meet my mother? You must have; she was always getting done over."

"At the beauty shop? Yes," Ivy replied, opening the door to a closet.

"Wonderful woman, isn't she?" His words were heavy with sarcasm. "Loves everyone. Never thinks of herself."

"I was young when I met her," Ivy said tactfully.

"I was young, too."

"Gregory . . . I've been wanting to say this. I know it must be hard for you, watching my mother move into your mother's room, having Philip and me take over space that was once yours. I don't blame you for—"

"For being glad that you're here?" he interrupted. "I am. I'm counting on you and Philip to keep the old man on his best behavior. He knows others are watching him and his new family. Now he's got to be the *good* and *loving* papa. Let me help you with that."

Ivy had picked up her box of angels. "No, really, Gregory, I can handle this myself."

He reached in his pocket for a penknife and slit the tape on the carton. "What's in it?"

"Ivy's angels," said Philip.

"The boy speaks!"

Philip pressed his lips together.

"Soon enough, you won't be able to shut him up," Ivy said. Then she opened the box and began to take out her carefully wrapped statues.

Tony came out first. Then an angel carved out of soft gray stone. Then her favorite, her water angel, a fragile porcelain figure painted in a swirl of blue-green.

Gregory watched as she unwrapped fifteen statues and set them on a shelf. His eyes were bright with amusement. "You don't take this stuff seriously, do you?"

"What do you mean by seriously?" she asked.

"You don't really believe in angels."

"I do," said Ivy.

He picked up the water angel and made her zoom around the room.

"Put her down!" Philip cried. "She's Ivy's favorite."

Gregory landed her facedown on a pillow.

"You're mean!"

"He's just playing, Philip," Ivy said, and calmly retrieved the angel.

Gregory lay back on the bed. "Do you pray to them?" he asked.

"Yes. To the angels, not the statues," she explained.

"And what wonderful things have these angels done for you? Have they captured Tristan's heart?"

Ivy glanced at him with surprise. "No. But then, I didn't pray for that."

Gregory laughed softly.

"Do you know Tristan?" Philip asked.

"Since first grade," Gregory replied, then lazily extended an arm toward the cat. Ella rolled away from him.

"He was the good kid on my Little League team," Gregory said, pulling himself up so he could reach Ella. She rose at the same time and walked to the other end of the bed. "He was the good kid on *every* team," Gregory said. He reached again for Ella.

The cat hissed. Ivy saw the color rising in Gregory's cheeks.

"Don't take it personally, Gregory," Ivy said. "Just let Ella be for a while. Cats often play hard to get."

"Like some girls I know," he remarked. "Come here, girl." He thrust his hand toward her. The cat raised a quick black paw, claws extended.

"Let her come to you," Ivy warned.

But Gregory took the cat by the scruff of the neck and pulled her upward.

"Don't!" Ivy cried.

He pushed his other hand up under her belly. Ella bit him hard on the wrist.

"Shoot!" He threw Ella across the room.

Philip ran for the cat. The cat ran to Ivy. She scooped her up in her arms. Ella's tail switched back and forth; she was angry rather than hurt. Gregory watched her, the color still high in his cheeks.

"Ella's a street kitten," Ivy told him, fighting to keep her own temper. "When I found her, she was a little bit of fur backed against a brick wall, holding her own against a big, torn-up tom. I tried to tell you. You can't come on to her that way. She doesn't trust people easily."

"Maybe you should teach her to," Gregory said. "*You* trust me, don't you?" He gave her one of his crooked, questioning smiles.

Ivy put down Ella. The cat sat under the chair and glowered at Gregory. At the sound of footsteps in the hall, she scooted under the bed.

Andrew stood in the doorway. "How's everything?" he asked.

"Fine," Ivy lied.

"It stinks," said Philip.

Andrew blinked, then nodded graciously. "Well, then," he said, "we'll have to try to make things better. Do you think we can?"

Philip just stared at him.

Andrew turned to Ivy. "Did you happen to

53

open that door yet?" Ivy followed his glance to Gregory's secret steps. "The light for the upstairs is on the left side," he told her.

Apparently he wanted her to investigate. Ivy opened the door and turned on the light. Philip, growing curious, slipped under her arm and scooted up the steps.

"Wow!" he shouted from above them. "Wow!"

Ivy glanced at Andrew. At the sound of Philip's excited voice, his face flushed with pleasure. Gregory stared intently out the window.

"Ivy, come see!"

Ivy hurried up the steps. She expected to see Nintendo, or Power Rangers, or maybe a life-size Don Mattingly. Instead she discovered a baby grand piano, a CD and tape player, and two cabinets filled with her musical scores. An album cover with Ella Fitzgerald's face was framed on the wall. The rest of her father's old jazz records were stored next to a cherrywood phonograph.

"If there is anything missing . . ." Andrew began. He was standing next to her, puffing a little from the steps, looking hopeful. Gregory had come halfway up, just far enough to see.

"Thanks!" was all Ivy could say. "Thanks!"

"This is cool, Ivy," Philip said.

"And it's for all three of us to share," she told him, glad that he was too excited to remember to sulk. Then she turned to speak to Gregory, but he had disappeared.

Dinner that night seemed to last forever. The lavishness of Andrew's gifts, the music room for Ivy and a well-stocked playroom for Philip, was both overwhelming and embarrassing. Since Philip, growing moody once more, had decided he would not speak at all at dinner—"Maybe never again," he'd told Ivy with a pout—it was up to her to express their gratitude to Andrew. But in doing so, she walked a tightrope: when Andrew asked a second time if there was anything else she and Philip wanted, she saw how Gregory's hands tensed.

In the middle of dessert, Suzanne telephoned. Ivy made the mistake of picking up the call in the hall outside the dining room. Suzanne was hoping for an invitation to the house that evening. Ivy told her the next day would be better.

"But I'm all dressed!" Suzanne complained.

"Of course you are," Ivy replied, "it's only seven-thirty."

"I meant dressed to come over."

"Gee, Suzanne," Ivy said, playing dumb, "you don't have to wear anything special to visit *me*."

"What's Gregory doing tonight?"

"I don't know. I haven't asked him."

"Well, find out! Find out her name and where she lives," Suzanne ordered, "and what she's wearing and where they go. If we don't know her, find out what she looks like. I just know he has a date," she wailed, "he must!"

Ivy had expected this. But she was worn out by the childishness of Philip and Gregory; she didn't feel like listening to the whining of Suzanne. "I've got to go now."

"I'll die if it's Twinkie Hammonds. Do you think it's Twinkie Hammonds?"

"I don't know. Gregory hasn't told me. Listen, I've got to go."

"Ivy, wait! You haven't told me anything yet."

Ivy sighed. "I'll be taking my usual lunch break at work tomorrow. Call Beth and meet me at the mall, okay?"

"Okay, but, Ivy—"

"I'd better get going now," Ivy said, "or else I'll miss my chance to hide in the trunk of Gregory's car." She hung up.

"So, how's Suzanne?" Gregory asked. He was leaning against the frame of the door that led into the dining room, his head cocked, smiling.

"Fine."

"What's she doing tonight?"

The laughter in his eyes told her that he had overheard the conversation, and that this was a tease, not sincere interest in the information.

"I didn't ask her and she hasn't told me. But if you two would like to talk it over with each other—"

He laughed, then touched Ivy on the tip of her nose. "Funny," he said. "I hope we keep you."

5

It was a relief to go to work Saturday morning, a relief to be back in territory that Ivy knew. Greentree Mall was in the next town over but drew high-school kids from all the surrounding towns. Most of them cruised the stores and hung around the food court. 'Tis the Season, where Ivy had worked for the last year and a half, was directly across from the food court.

The shop was owned by two old sisters, whose selection of costumes, decorations, paperware, and knickknacks was as eccentric as their style of business. Lillian and Betty rarely returned merchandise, and it was as if all the seasons and holidays had run into one another in one small corner of the world. Vampire costumes hung with the Stars and Stripes; Easter chickens roosted next to miniature plastic menorahs, pine-cone turkeys, and Vulcan ears from the last Trekkie convention.

Just before one o'clock on Saturday, while waiting for Suzanne and Beth to arrive, Ivy was glancing over the day's special orders. As always, they were scrawled on Post-it notes and stuck on the wall. Ivy read one of the tags twice, then pulled it off. Couldn't be, she thought, couldn't be. Maybe there were two of them. Two guys named Tristan Carruthers?

"Lillian, what does this mean? 'For pick-up: Bl Blup Wh and 25 pnc.'?"

Lillian squinted at the paper. She had bifocals, but they usually rode her chest at the end of a necklace.

"Well, twenty-five plates, napkins, and cups, you know that. Ah yes, for Tristan Carruthers—an order for the swim team party. Blue blow-up whale. I've already got it ready. He called to check on the order this morning."

"Trist—Mr. Carruthers called?"

Now Lillian reached for her glasses. Settling them on her nose, she looked hard at Ivy. "Mr. Carruthers? He didn't call you Miss Lyons," she said.

"Why would he call me anything?" Ivy wondered aloud. "I mean, why did my name come up?"

"He asked what hours you were working. I told him you take lunch between one and one-forty-five, but otherwise you'd be here till six." She smiled at Ivy. "And I put in a few good words for you, dear."

"A few good words?"

"I told him what a lovely girl you are, and what a shame it is that someone like you couldn't find a deserving gentleman friend."

Ivy winced, but Lillian had removed her glasses again, so she didn't notice.

"He came into the shop last week to place the order," Lillian continued. "He's quite a chunk."

"Hunk, Lillian."

"Pardon me?"

"Tristan's quite a *hunk*."

"Well, she's finally admitting it!" said Suzanne, striding into the store. Beth came in behind her. "Good work, Lillian!" The old woman winked, and Ivy stuck the Post-it back on the wall. She began to dig in her pockets for money.

"Don't expect to eat," Suzanne warned her. "This is an interrogation."

Twenty minutes later, Beth was just about finished with her burrito. Suzanne had made inroads on her teriyaki chicken. Ivy's pizza remained untouched.

"How should I know?" she was saying, waving her arms with frustration. "I didn't get into his medicine cupboard!" They had hashed and rehashed and interpreted and reinterpreted every detail that Ivy had observed about Gregory's room.

"Well, I guess you've only been there one night," Suzanne said. "But tonight, maybe. You must find out where he's going tonight. Does he have a curfew? Does he—"

Ivy picked up an egg roll and stuffed it in Suzanne's mouth. "It's Beth's turn to talk," she said.

"Oh, that's all right," Beth said. "This is interesting."

Ivy opened Beth's folder. "Why don't you read one of your new stories," she said, "before Suzanne makes me totally crazy."

Beth glanced at Suzanne, then cheerfully pulled out a sheaf of papers. "I'm going to use this new one for drama club on Monday. I've been experimenting with *in medias res.* That means starting right in the middle of the action."

Ivy nodded to her encouragingly and took the first bite out of her pizza.

"'She clutched the gun to her breast,'" Beth read. "'Hard and blue, cold and unyielding. Photos of him. Frail and faded photos of him—of him with *her*—torn-up, tear-soaked,

61

salt-crusted photos lay scattered by her chair. She'd wash them away with her own blood—'"

"Beth, Beth," Suzanne cut in. "This is lunch. Something a pound lighter?"

Beth agreeably shuffled through the papers and began again. "'She clutched his hand to her breast. Warm and damp, soft and supple—'"

"His hand or her breast?" Suzanne interrupted.

"Quiet," said Ivy.

"'—a hand that could hold her very soul, a hand that could lift'—a whale, a blue plastic whale, I think. What *else* could that be?"

Ivy turned around quickly and looked across the mall to the shop. Betty was holding up a big piece of blue plastic and chatting away to Tristan. Lillian was standing behind Tristan at the shop entrance, beckoning furiously to her. Ivy glanced at her watch. It was 1:25, halfway through her lunch break. "She wants you," said Beth.

Ivy shook her head at Lillian, but Lillian kept waving at her.

"Go get 'im, girl," said Suzanne.

"No."

"Oh, come on, Ivy."

"You don't understand. He knows I'm on lunch break. He's avoiding me."

"Maybe," said Suzanne, "but I've never let a thing like that stop me."

Now Tristan had turned around and, noticing Lillian's imitation of a highway flagman, surveyed the crowd in the food court until his eyes came to rest on Ivy. Meanwhile, Betty had managed to hook the inflatable whale up to the store's helium canister.

"Yo!" exclaimed Beth as the whale took on a life of its own, growing like a blue thundercloud behind Tristan and Lillian. Betty disappeared on the other side of it. She must have cut it loose suddenly, for it rose to the ceiling. Tristan had to jump to nab it. Beth and Suzanne started laughing. Lillian shook her finger at Ivy, then turned to talk to Tristan.

"I wonder what she's saying to him," Beth said.

"A few good words," mumbled Ivy.

Minutes later Tristan emerged from the shop clutching the bag of party stuff, which had been tied up by the sisters with a fancy blue bow. The whale trailed above and behind him. He kept his eyes straight ahead and marched toward the mall exit. Suzanne called out to him.

Bellowed, actually. He couldn't pretend not to hear her. He looked in their direction and then, with a rather grim expression on his face, made his way toward them. Several small children followed him as if he were the Pied Piper.

"Hi," he said stiffly. "Suzanne. Beth. Ivy. Nice to see you."

"Nice to see *you*," Suzanne said, then eyed the whale. "Who's this? He's kind of cute. Newest member of the swim team?"

Ivy noticed that Tristan's knuckles were white on the hand that held the whale's string. Muscles all the way up his arm were tense and bulging. Behind him, the kids were jumping up and down, punching at the whale.

"Actually, the newest member of my act," he said, and turned to Ivy. "You've seen part of it— the carrot and shrimp-tail routine I do? I don't know what it is. Eight-year-olds find me irresistible." He glanced back at the kids. "Sorry, got to go now."

"Noooo!" the kids cried. He let them take a few more bats at the whale, then left, weaving his way quickly through the Saturday shoppers.

"Well!" huffed Suzanne. "Well!" She poked Ivy with her chopstick. "You could have said something! Really, girl, I don't know *what* is wrong with you."

"What did you want me to say?"

"Anything! Something! It doesn't matter— just let him know it's all right to talk to you."

Ivy swallowed hard. She couldn't understand why Tristan did some of the things he did. He made her so self-conscious.

"You always feel self-conscious at first," Beth said, as if reading Ivy's thoughts. "But sooner or later you'll figure out how to act around each other."

Suzanne leaned forward. "Your problem is that you take it all too seriously, Ivy. Romance is a game, just a game."

Ivy sighed and glanced at her watch. "I've got ten more minutes on break. Beth, how about finishing your love story?"

Suzanne tapped Ivy's arm. "You've got two more months of school," she said. "How about starting yours?"

6

Ivy stood barefoot on the clammy floor, curling up her toes. The humidity and the pool's strong smell of chlorine invaded the locker room. Metal doors slammed and the cinder-block room echoed like a cave. Everything about the pool area gave her the creeps.

The other girls in the drama club were checking out one another's suits, rehearsing their lines, and giggling self-consciously.

Suzanne laid a hand on Ivy's shoulder. "You all right?"

"I can handle this."

"You're sure?" Suzanne didn't sound convinced.

"I know my lines," said Ivy, "and all we have to do is jump up and down on the diving board." On the *high* diving board, at the *deep* end, without falling in, Ivy thought to herself.

Suzanne persisted. "Listen, Ivy, I know you're McCardell's star, but don't you think you should mention to him that you don't know how to swim and are terrified of water?"

"I told you I can do this," Ivy said, then pushed through the swinging locker room door, her legs feeling like soft rubber beneath her.

She lined up with eleven girls and three guys along the pool's edge. Beth stood on one side of Ivy, Suzanne on the other. Ivy gazed down into the luminescent blue-green pool. It's just water, she told herself, nothing more than stuff to drink. And it's not even deep at this end.

Beth touched her on the arm. "Well, I guess Suzanne is pleased. You invited Gregory."

"Gregory? Of course I didn't!" Ivy turned swiftly to Suzanne.

Suzanne shrugged. "I wanted to give him a preview of coming attractions. There'll be lots of places to sunbathe on that ridge of yours."

"You do look great in your suit," Beth told her.

Ivy fumed. Suzanne knew how hard this was for her, without adding Gregory to the scenario. She could have restrained herself just this once.

Gregory wasn't alone in the bleachers. His friends Eric and Will were watching, as well as some other juniors and seniors who had slipped away from their projects during the activity period. All of the guys watched with intense interest as the girls in the group did their stretching exercises.

Then the class walked and trotted around the perimeter of the pool, performing their vocal drills.

"I want to hear every consonant, every *p, d,* and *t,*" Mr. McCardell called out to them, his own voice amazingly distinct in the huge echo chamber of the pool. "Margaret, Courtney, Suzanne, this isn't a beauty pageant," he hollered. "*Just walk.*"

That elicited some soft booing from the stands.

"And for heaven's sake, Sam, stop bouncing!"

The audience snickered.

When the students had finished several circuits, they gathered at the deep end of the pool, beneath the high dive.

"Eyes here," their teacher commanded. "You're not with me." Leaning close to them, he said, "This is a lesson in enunciation *and* concentration. I'll find it unforgivable if any one of you lets those groundlings distract you."

At that, nearly everyone in the class glanced toward the stands. The pool door opened, and more spectators entered, all of them guys.

"Are we ready? Are we preparing ourselves?"

For the exercise, each student had to memorize at least twenty-five lines of poetry or prose, something about love or death—"the two great themes of life and drama," Mr. McCardell had said.

Ivy had patched together two early-English love lyrics, one funny and one sad. She silently ran over their lines. She thought she knew them by heart, but when the first student climbed the thin metal ladder, every word went out of her head. Ivy's pulse began to race as if she were the one on the ladder. She took deep breaths.

"Are you okay?" Beth whispered.

"Tell him, Ivy!" Suzanne urged. "Explain to McCardell how you feel."

Ivy shook her head. "I'm fine."

The first three students delivered their lines mechanically, but all of them kept their balance, bouncing up and down on the board. Then Sam fell in. With arms wheeling like some huge, strange bird, he came crashing down into the water.

Ivy swallowed hard.

Mr. McCardell called her name.

She climbed the ladder, slowly and steadily, rung by rung, her heart pounding against her ribs. Her arms felt stronger than her shaky legs. She used them to pull herself up onto the board, then stopped. Below her the water danced, dark wavelets with fluorescent sparkles.

Ivy focused on the end of the board, as she had been taught to do on a balance beam, and took three steps. She felt the board give beneath her weight. Her stomach dropped with it, but she kept on walking.

"You may begin," said Mr. McCardell.

Ivy turned her thoughts inward for a moment, trying to find her lines, trying to remember the pictures she had imagined when she first read the poetry. She knew that if she did this simply as an exercise, she would not get through it. She had to perform, she had to lose herself to the poems' emotions.

She found the first few words of the humorous poem, and suddenly in her mind's eye saw the pictures she needed: a glittering bride, stunned guests, and a shower of rolling vegetables. Far below her, her audience laughed as she recited lines about the silliness of love. Then, continuing her jumping motion, she found the slower, sadder rhythm of the second poem:

> Western wind, when will thou blow,
> The small rain down can rain?
> Christ, if my love were in my arms
> And I in my bed again!

She jumped for two beats more, then stood still at the end of the board, catching her breath. Suddenly applause rang out. She had done it!

When the cheers died down, Mr. McCardell said, "Nice enough," which was high praise from him.

"Thank you, sir," Ivy replied. Then she tried to turn around for the walk back.

As she started to turn she felt her knees buckle, and she quickly stiffened herself. Don't look down.

But she had to see where she was stepping. She took a deep breath and attempted to turn again.

"Ivy, is there a problem?" Mr. McCardell asked.

"She's afraid of water," Suzanne blurted. "And she can't swim."

Below Ivy the pool seemed to rock, its edges blurred. She tried to focus on the board. She couldn't. The water came rushing at her, ready to swallow her up. Then it receded, dropping away, far, far below her. Ivy swayed on her feet. One knee went down.

"Oh!" The cry echoed up from the spectators.

Her other knee went down and slipped off the board. Ivy clung with the desperation of a cat. She dangled, half on, half off the board.

"Somebody help her!" cried Suzanne.

Water angel, Ivy prayed silently. Water angel, don't let me fall. You helped me once. Please, angel . . .

Then Ivy felt movement in the board. It trembled in her arms. Her hands were damp and slippery. Just drop, she told herself. Trust your angel. Your angel won't let you drown. Water angel, she prayed a third time, but her arms wouldn't let go. The board continued to vibrate. Her hands were slipping.

"Ivy."

She turned her face at the sound of his voice, scraping her cheek on the board. Tristan had climbed the ladder and was standing at the other end. "Everything is going to be all right, Ivy."

Then he started toward her. The fiberglass plank flexed under his weight.

"Don't!" Ivy cried, clinging desperately to the board. "Don't bend it. Please! I'm afraid."

"I can help you. Trust me."

Her arms ached. Her head felt light, her skin cold and prickly. Beneath her, the water swirled dizzily.

"Listen to me, Ivy. You're not going to be able to keep holding on that way. Roll on your side a little. Roll, okay? Get your right arm free. Come on. I know you can do it."

Ivy slowly shifted her weight. For a moment she thought she was going to roll right off the board. Her freed arm waved frantically.

"You got it. You got it," he said.

He was right. She had a good hold, both hands squarely on the board.

"Now inch up. Pull yourself all the way onto the board. That's the way." His voice was steady and sure. "Which knee is your favorite knee?" he asked.

She frowned up at him.

"Are you right-kneed or left-kneed?" He was smiling at her.

"Uh, right-kneed, I guess."

"Loosen up your right hand, then. And pull your right knee up, tuck it under you." She did. A moment later both knees were under her.

"Now crawl to me."

She looked down at the rocking bowl of water.

"Come to me, Ivy."

The distance was only eight feet—it looked like eight miles. She made her way slowly along the board. Then she felt a hand gripping hard on each arm. He stood up, pulling her up with him, and quickly turned her around. Ivy went limp with relief.

"Okay, I'm right behind you now. We'll take one step at a time. I'm right here." He began to move down the ladder.

One step at a time, Ivy repeated to herself.

If only her legs would stop shaking. Then she felt his hand lightly on her ankle, guiding it down to the metal rung. At last they stood together at the bottom.

Mr. McCardell glanced away from her, obviously uncomfortable.

"Thank you," Ivy said quietly to Tristan.

Then she rushed into the locker room before Tristan or the others could see her frightened tears.

In the parking lot that afternoon, Suzanne tried to talk Ivy into coming home with her to the Goldstein house.

"Thanks, but I'm tired," Ivy said. "I think I should go . . . home." It was still strange to think of the Baines house as home.

"Well, why don't we just drive around some first?" Suzanne suggested. "I know a great cappuccino place where none of the kids go, at least none from our school. We can talk without being interrupted."

"I don't need to talk, Suzanne. I'm okay. Really. But if you want to just hang out, you can come home with *me*."

"I don't think that would be a good idea."

Ivy cocked her head. "You would think you were the one who'd been stranded up there on the diving board."

"It felt like it," said Suzanne.

"If I didn't know better, I'd think you'd fallen from the ladder and hit your head on the concrete. I just invited you to Gregory's house."

Suzanne fiddled with her lipstick, rolling it up and down, up and down in its case. "That's just it. You know how I am, Ivy—like a bloodhound on the hunt. I can't help myself. If he's there, I'll get completely distracted. And right now you need my attention."

"But I don't need anybody's attention! I had a bad time in drama club and—"

"Got rescued."

"Got rescued—"

"By Tristan."

"By Tristan, and now—"

"You'll live happily ever after," said Suzanne.

"Now I'll go home, and if you want to come with me and start baying at Gregory, fine. It will keep us all entertained."

Suzanne debated for a moment, then stretched her freshly darkened lips. "Did I get it on my teeth?"

"If you didn't talk constantly, you wouldn't have this problem," Ivy said, and pointed to a smudge of red. "Right there."

When they arrived home, Gregory's BMW was in the driveway. "Well, we're all in luck," said Ivy.

But when they got inside the house, Ivy could hear her mother's voice, high and excited, being answered quickly each time by Gregory's. She and Suzanne exchanged glances, then followed the sound of the voices to Andrew's office.

"Is something wrong?" asked Ivy.

"That's what's wrong!" said her mother, pointing to a silk-covered chair. Its back hung in shreds.

"Ouch!" Ivy exclaimed. "What happened to it?"

"Perhaps my father was filing his nails," Gregory suggested.

"It's Andrew's favorite chair," said Maggie. Her cheeks were quite pink. Her sprayed hair was falling out of its twist in grasslike wisps. "And this fabric is not exactly cheap, Ivy."

"Well, Mother, I didn't do it!"

"Let me check your nails," said Gregory.

Suzanne laughed.

"Ella did it," Maggie said.

"Ella!" Ivy shook her head. "That's impossible! Ella's never scratched anything in her life."

"Ella doesn't like Andrew," Philip said. He had been standing quietly in the corner of the room. "She did it because she doesn't like Andrew."

Maggie whirled around. Ivy caught her

mother by the hand. "Easy," she said. Then she examined the back of the chair. Gregory watched her and examined the chair himself. It seemed to Ivy to be too finely shredded—a job too convincing for Philip to have pulled off. Ella must have been guilty.

"We're going to have to declaw her," said Maggie.

"No!"

"Ivy, there are too many valuable pieces of furniture in this house. They cannot be ruined. Ella will have to be declawed."

"I won't let you."

"She's just a cat."

"And this is just a piece of furniture," Ivy said, her voice cold and steely.

"It's that, or get rid of her."

Ivy folded her arms across her chest. She was two inches taller than her mother.

"Ivy—" She could see her mother's eyes misting over. That was what she had been like for the past few months, emotional, pleading, insisting with tears. "Ivy, this is a new life, these are new ways for all of us. You told me yourself: For all the good things that are happening, this isn't a fairy-tale ending. We all have to try to make it work."

"Where is Ella now?" Ivy asked.

"In your bedroom. I closed the hall door,

and the attic one too, so she wouldn't ruin anything else."

Ivy turned to Gregory. "Would you get Suzanne something to drink?"

"Of course," he said.

Then Ivy went up to her room. She sat for a long time, cradling Ella in her lap and gazing up at her water angel.

"What do I do now, angel?" she prayed. "What do I do now? Don't tell me to give up Ella! I can't give her up. I can't!"

In the end, she did. In the end, Ivy couldn't take the outdoors away from Ella. She couldn't leave her fierce little street cat vulnerable to anything that would take a swipe at her. Though it just about broke her heart, and Philip's too, she posted the adoption ad on the school bulletin board Thursday afternoon.

Thursday night she got a call. Philip was in her room doing his homework and picked up the phone. He somberly handed it over to her. "It's a man," he said. "He wants to adopt Ella."

Ivy frowned and took the receiver. "Hello?"

"Hi. How are you?" the caller asked.

"Fine," Ivy replied stiffly. Did it matter how she was? She immediately disliked this person— because he hoped to take away Ella.

"Good. Uh . . . did you find a home for your cat?"

"No," she said.

"I'd like to have her."

Ivy blinked hard. She didn't want Philip to see her cry. She should be glad and relieved that someone wanted a full-grown cat.

"Are you there?" asked the caller.

"Yes."

"I'd take good care of her, feed her and wash her."

"You don't wash cats."

"I'd learn what I have to do," he said. "I think she'd like it here. It's a comfortable place."

Ivy nodded silently.

"Hello?"

She turned her back on Philip. "Listen," she said into the phone. "Ella means a lot to me. If you don't mind, I'd like to see your home myself and talk to you in person."

"I don't mind at all!" the caller replied cheerfully. "Let me give you my address."

She copied it down. "And who is this?" she asked.

"Tristan."

79

7

"But you're a dog person," Gary said on Friday afternoon. "You've always been a dog person."

"I think my parents will enjoy a cat," Tristan replied. He moved quickly around the living room, clearing piles of stuff off the chairs: his mother's pediatrics journals, his father's hospital chapel schedules and stacks of photocopied prayers, his own swim schedules and old copies of *Sports Illustrated*, the previous night's tub of chicken. His parents would wonder why he had gone to all the trouble. Usually the three of them sat on the floor to read and eat.

Gary was watching him and frowning. "You think your *parents* will enjoy it? Does the cat have a disease? Does it have a religion? If your mother the doctor can't cure it and your father the minister can't pray for and counsel it—"

"All homes need a pet," Tristan cut in.

"In homes where there's a cat, the *people* are the pets. I'm telling you, Tristan, cats have minds of their own. They're worse than girls. If you think Ivy can drive you crazy— Wait a minute . . . wait a minute . . ." Gary tapped his fingers on the table. "I remember an ad on the bulletin board."

"That's nice," Tristan said, and handed his friend his gym bag. "You said you had to get home early today."

Gary dropped his bag. He had figured out what was up. "And miss this? I was there the last time you made a fool of yourself; why shouldn't I stay for the fun this time?" He threw himself down on the rug in front of the fireplace.

"You're really enjoying my misery, aren't you?" Tristan murmured.

Gary rolled over on his back and put his hands behind his head. "Tristan, me and the guys have been watching you get all the girls for the last three years—no, for the last seven; you were hot even in fifth grade. Darn right I'm enjoying it!"

Tristan grimaced, then turned his attention to a coffee stain that seemed to have tripled in size since he'd last noticed it. He had no idea how to get something like that out of a rug.

He wondered if Ivy would find his family's old frame house small and worn and unbelievably cluttered.

"So, what's the deal?" Gary asked. "One date for taking her cat? Maybe one date for each week you keep it," he suggested.

"Her friend Suzanne said she's very attached to this cat." Tristan smiled, rather pleased with himself. "I'm offering visitation rights."

Gary snorted. "What happens when Ivy doesn't miss the old furball anymore?"

"She'll miss me," Tristan said, sounding confident.

The doorbell rang. His confidence evaporated.

"Quick, how do you pick up a cat?"

"Buy her a drink."

"I'm serious!"

"By the tail."

"You're kidding!"

"Yup. I'm kidding."

The doorbell rang again. Tristan hurried to answer it. Was it his imagination, or did Ivy blush a little when he opened the door? Her mouth was definitely rosy. Her hair shone like a halo of gold, and her green eyes made him think of warm, tropical seas.

"I've brought Ella," she said.

"Ella?"

"My cat."

Looking down, he saw all kinds of animal paraphernalia on the porch beside her.

"Oh, *Ella!* Great. Great." Why did she always reduce him to one-word sentences?

"You're still interested, aren't you?" A small line of worry creased her brow.

"Oh, he's interested all right," Gary replied, rising up behind Tristan.

Ivy stepped into the house and looked about without putting down her cat carrier.

"I'm Gary. I've seen you around a lot at school."

Ivy nodded and smiled somewhat distantly. "You were at the wedding, too."

"Right. Me and Tristan. I'm the one who made it all the way through dessert before being fired."

Ivy smiled again, a friendlier smile this time, then she got back to business.

"Ella's litter pan is outside," she said to Tristan. "And some cans of food. I also brought her basket and cushion, but she never uses them."

Tristan nodded. Ivy's hair was blowing in the draft from the door. He wanted to touch it. He wanted to brush it off her cheek and kiss her.

"How would you feel about sharing your bed?" she asked.

Tristan blinked. "Excuse me?"

"He'd love to!" Gary said.

Tristan shot him a look.

"Good," said Ivy, failing to notice Gary's wink. "Ella can be a pillow hog, but all you have to do is roll her over."

Gary laughed out loud, then he and Tristan brought in the pile of stuff.

"Are you a cat person?" Ivy asked Gary.

"No," he replied, "but maybe there's hope for me." He leaned down to peer into the carrier. "I mean, look how fast Tristan converted. Hello, Ella. We're going to have a great time playing together."

"Too bad you'll have to wait till next time," said Tristan. "Gary was just leaving," he told Ivy.

Gary straightened up with a look of mock surprise. "I'm leaving? So soon?"

"Not soon enough," Tristan said, holding open the front door.

"Okay, okay. Catch you later, Ella. Maybe we can hunt mice together."

When Gary left, the room grew suddenly quiet. Tristan couldn't think of anything to say. He had a list of questions—somewhere—behind the sofa where all the other stuff was jammed.

But Ivy didn't seem to expect conversation. She unlatched the door of the cat carrier and pulled out Ella.

The cat was funny-looking, mostly black, but with one white foot, a tip of white on her tail, and a splash of it on her face.

"Okay, baby," Ivy said, holding Ella in her arms, stroking her softly around the ears.

Ella blinked her huge green eyes at Tristan, happily soaking up Ivy's attention.

I can't believe I'm jealous of a cat, Tristan thought.

When Ivy finally set Ella on the floor, Tristan held out his hand. The cat gave him a snooty look and walked away.

"You have to let her come to you," Ivy advised him. "Ignore her, for days, for weeks, if necessary. When she gets lonely enough, she'll come around on her own."

Would Ivy ever?

Tristan picked up a yellow pad. "How about giving me feeding instructions?"

She had already typed them up for him. "And here are Ella's medical records, and here's the list of shots she gets regularly, and the vet's number."

She seemed in a rush to get it over with.

"And here are her toys." Ivy's voice faltered

"This is hard for you, isn't it?" he said gently.

"And here's her brush; she loves to be brushed."

"But not washed," Tristan said.

Ivy bit her lip. "You don't know anything about cats, do you?"

"I'll learn, I promise. She'll be good for me, and I'll be good for her. Of course, you can visit her as much as you like, Ivy. She'll still be your cat. She'll just be my cat too. You can come see her whenever you want."

"No," Ivy said firmly. "No."

"No?" His heart stopped. He was still sitting upright holding a pile of kitty stuff, but he was sure he'd just had a cardiac arrest.

"It will only mix her up," Ivy explained. "And I don't think—I don't think I can stand to."

He longed to reach out to touch her then, to take one of her slender hands in his, but he didn't dare. Instead he pretended to study the little pink brush and waited for Ivy to regain her composure.

Ella came over to sniff her brush, then pushed her head against it. Tristan gently ran it along her flank.

"She likes it best around her head," Ivy said. She took his hand and guided it. "Under her chin. And her cheeks—that's where her scent glands are, the ones she uses for marking things. I think she likes you, Tristan."

She took her hand away. Tristan continued to brush Ella. The cat suddenly rolled over on her back.

Ivy laughed. "Well, well! You little tramp!"

With his hand Tristan rubbed her belly. The fur was luxuriously long and soft.

"I wonder why cats don't like water," he mused. "If you threw one in a pool, would it swim?"

"Don't you dare!" Ivy said. "Don't you dare do that!"

The cat leaped to its feet and scooted under a chair.

Tristan looked at Ivy with surprise. "Of course I wouldn't. I was just wondering."

She dropped her eyes. Color crept into her cheeks.

"Is that what happened to you, Ivy?"

When she didn't answer, he tried again. "What made you afraid of water?" he asked quietly. "Something from when you were a little kid?"

Ivy wouldn't look at him. "I owe you big time," she said, "for getting me down from that board."

"You don't owe me anything. I was just asking because I was trying to understand. Swimming is my life. It's hard for me to imagine what it's like not to love water."

"I don't see how you could understand," Ivy

said. "Water to you is like wind to a bird. It lets you fly. At least that's how it looks. It's hard for me to imagine how that feels."

"What made you afraid of it?" he persisted. "Who made you afraid of it?"

She thought for a moment. "I don't even remember his name. One of my mother's boyfriends. She had a lot of them and some of them were nice. But he was mean. He took us to a friend's pool. I was four, I think. I didn't know how to swim and didn't want to go in the water. I guess I got annoying after a while, hanging on to Mom."

She swallowed and glanced up at Tristan.

"And?" he said softly.

"Mom went inside for a few minutes, to help with sandwiches or something. He grabbed hold of me. I knew what he was going to do and started kicking and screaming, but Mom didn't hear me. He dragged me over to the pool's edge. 'Let's see if she'll swim!' he said, 'Let's see if the cat will swim!' He picked me up high and threw me in."

Tristan flinched, as if he were there, actually watching it.

"The water was way over my head," Ivy continued. "I floundered around, kicking and moving my arms, but I couldn't keep my face above water. I started choking on it, swallowing it. I couldn't get up for air."

Tristan stared at her, incredulous. "And this guy, did he jump in after you?"

"No." Ivy had risen to her feet and was moving around the room like a restless cat. Ella poked her head out to watch, a dust ball hanging from her whiskers.

"I'm pretty sure he was drunk," Ivy said. "Everything started getting blurry to me. Then dark. My arms and legs seemed so heavy, and my chest felt like it would burst. I prayed. For the first time in my life, I prayed to my guardian angel. Then I felt myself being lifted up, held above the water. My lungs stopped hurting, my eyes grew clear. I don't remember much about the angel, except that she was shining, and many colors, and beautiful."

Ivy glanced sideways at Tristan, then broke into a wide smile. She came back to him and sat on the floor again, facing him.

"It's okay. I don't expect you to believe me. Nobody else did. Apparently my mother had come out to see what was going on and her friend had turned around to speak to her, so no one saw how I made it back to the pool's edge They just figured that, thrown in, a kid would learn to swim." Her face was wistful. She was somewhere else again, still remembering.

"I'd like to believe in your angel," Tristan said. Then he shrugged. "Sorry." He had heard stories like it before. His father occasionally brought such tales home from the hospital. But it was just the way the human mind worked, he thought; it was the way certain minds respond in a crisis.

"You know, when I was up there on the board Monday," Ivy said, "I prayed to my water angel."

"But all you got was me," Tristan pointed out.

"Good enough," she replied, and laughed a little.

"Ivy—" He tried to still the tremor in his voice, not wanting her to know how much he was hoping. "I could teach you how to swim."

Her eyes opened wide.

"After school. The coach would let us in the pool."

Her hands, her eyes, everything about her was still and watching him.

"It's a great feeling, Ivy. Do you know what it's like to float on a lake, a circle of trees around you, a big blue bowl of sky above you? You're just lying on top of the water, sun sparkling at the tips of your fingers and toes. Do you know how it feels to swim in the ocean? To be swimming hard and have a wave catch you and effortlessly lift you up—"

Without realizing what he was doing, he put a hand on each arm and lifted her. Her skin was covered with goose bumps.

"Sorry," he said, letting her down quickly. "I'm sorry. I got carried away."

"It's okay," she said, but she wouldn't look at him again.

He wondered which she was more afraid of, the water or him.

Probably him, he thought, and he didn't know what to do about it. "I'd make it fun, just like when I teach the kids at summer camp," Tristan said encouragingly. "Think about it, okay?"

She nodded.

Clearly he made her uncomfortable. He wished he could apologize for plowing into her in the hall, for showing up at her mother's wedding, for calling her about her cat. He wanted to promise her that he wouldn't bother her anymore, hoping that would put her at ease. But she suddenly looked so confused and tired; it seemed best not to say anything else.

"I'll be real good to Ella," he told her. "If something changes and you want her back, give me a call. And if you decide that you do want to visit her, I don't have to be around. Okay?"

Ivy looked up at him wonderingly.

"So," he said, standing up. "I'm the cook Tuesdays and Fridays. I'd better start dinner."

"What are you fixing?" Ivy asked.

"Liver bits and gravy. Oh, no, sorry, that's Ella's can."

It was a weak joke, but she smiled.

"Stay and play with Ella as long as you like," he told her.

"Thank you."

Then he headed toward the kitchen to give her some time alone with the cat. But before he had gotten to the doorway he heard her say, "Good-bye, Ella." A moment later, the front door clicked shut behind her.

When Ivy emerged from the locker room, Tristan was already in the water. Coach had let her into the locked pool area. She had expected the older man to stare at her in disbelief—"You mean you don't know how to swim?" But his face, which was long and lined like a raisin, was kind and unquestioning. He greeted her, then retreated to his office.

It had taken Ivy a week to decide to do this. She had swum in her dreams, for miles some nights. When she told Tristan she wanted to learn, his eyes had lit up. Ivy was pretty sure she had successfully discouraged any romantic interest he had in her; according to Suzanne, he was dating two other girls. But she felt as if he was her friend. Getting her down from the board, taking in Ella, helping her face her greatest fear—he was there when she needed him, the way no other guy had been, the way a real friend would be.

Now she watched him doing laps. The water flowed past his muscular body; it lifted him up as he moved swiftly and powerfully through it. When he swam the butterfly, his arms pulling up out of the water like wings, he was visual music—strong, rhythmic, graceful.

Ivy watched for several minutes, then came back to the reason she was there. She walked to the pool's edge at the shallow end and stared down at it. Then she sat down and slipped in her legs. It was warm. Soothing. Still, she was cold all over. She gritted her teeth and slid off the side. The water rose to just below her shoulders. She imagined it inching up over her throat, her mouth. She closed her eyes and gripped the side of the pool, trying to stop the fear rising within her.

Water angel, she prayed, don't let go of me. I'm trusting you, angel. I'm in your hands.

Tristan stopped swimming. "You're here," he said. "You're in."

He looked so pleased that for a moment, a very brief moment, she forgot her fear.

"How are you doing?" he asked.

"Fine. You don't mind if I just stand here and shake, do you?"

"You'll warm up if you move around," he told her.

She glanced down at the water.

"Come on, let's take a walk." He took her

hand and walked her along the edge of the pool, as if they were walking the mall, though in the resistant water each step was in slow motion.

"Do you want me to tell you about Ella and the chaos she's creating at home?"

"Sure," said Ivy. "Did she find that tub of chicken wedged into your television cabinet?"

Tristan looked startled for a moment, then recovered. "Yes, right after she burrowed through all the stuff I'd crammed behind the sofa." He chattered on, telling her several Ella stories, walking her up and down the short end of the pool.

When they stopped, he said, "I think we'd better get some water on your face."

She had been dreading that.

He scooped handfuls of it up over her forehead and cheeks as if he were washing a baby.

"I do that in the shower," Ivy said tartly.

"Well, excuse me, Miss Advanced. We'll go on to the next step." He grinned at her. "Take a big breath. I want to see you looking at me under there. The chlorine will sting a little, but I want to see those big green eyes and little bubbles coming out of your nose. Suck in above the water, blow out below it. Got it? One, two, three." He pulled her down with him. Up and down they bobbed, he holding her down there a little longer each time, making faces at her.

Ivy came up to the surface, sputtering and choking.

"Now, if you can't follow a few simple directions . . ." he began.

"You're making me laugh!" said Ivy. "It's no fair when you make me laugh."

"All right. Now we get serious. Sort of."

He taught her how she would breathe when swimming, pretending the water was a pillow, turning her head to the side to breathe in. She practiced, gripping the side of the pool with her hands. Then he took her hands and pulled her through the water. She naturally started kicking her feet to keep them afloat behind her. It was tempting to pull her head up and look at him. Once Ivy did and found him smiling at her.

They worked on kicking for a while. After she practiced on the side, they played train. He had her grab his ankles, following behind him in the water, he swimming with his arms and she kicking her feet. It amazed her that he could pull her so swiftly with just the strength of his arms.

When they stopped, he asked her, "Are you getting tired? Do you want to sit up on the side for a few minutes?"

Ivy shook her head no. "If I get out, I don't know if I'll get in again."

"You've got guts," he said.

She laughed. "I'm standing in water just up to my shoulders and you call that guts?"

"Yup." He swam in a circle around her. "Ivy, everyone has something they're afraid of. You're one of the few people who face their fear. But then, I always knew you were the gutsy type. I knew from the first day, when I saw you striding across the cafeteria, that cheerleader, who was supposed to be leading you around, following."

"I was hungry," Ivy said. "And that was a bit of a performance."

"Well, you carried it off."

She smiled and he reflected her smile, his hazel eyes alight and lashes spangled with water drops.

"Okay," he said. "Want to float on your back?"

"No. But I will."

"It's easy." Tristan stretched back in the water and floated, looking entirely relaxed. "You see what I'm doing?"

Looking *awfully* good, she thought, then thanked her angels that he couldn't read minds as well as Beth.

"I keep my hips up, arch my back, then just let everything else go. You try it."

Ivy did, and sank. The old panic returned for a moment.

"You were sitting," he told her. "You let your seat drop down. Try again."

As she lay back again he slid an arm under her. "Easy now, don't fight it. Back arched. That's the way." He slipped his arm out from under her.

Ivy pulled her head up and started to sink again. She stood up angrily. Her wet hair was coming loose out of her ponytail holder and slapped against her neck.

Tristan laughed. "That's how I imagine Ella would look if she ever got wet."

"A little kid could do this," Ivy told him.

"Kids can do a lot of things," he replied, "because kids trust. The trick in swimming is not to fight the water. Go with it. Play with it. Give yourself over to it." He splashed her lightly. "How about trying again?"

She lay back. She felt his left arm under the arch in her back. With his right hand he gently eased her head back. The water lapped around her forehead and chin. Ivy closed her eyes and gave herself over to the water. She imagined being in the center of a lake, sunlight sparkling at her toes and fingertips.

When she opened her eyes, he was looking down at her. His face was like the sun, warming her, brightening the air around it. "I'm floating," she whispered.

"You're floating," he said softly, his face bending closer.

"Floating . . ." They read it off each other's lips, their faces close, so close—

"Tristan!"

Tristan straightened up and Ivy sank.

It was Coach, calling from the door of his office. "Sorry to toss you two out," he hollered, "but I got to head home in about ten minutes."

"No problem, Coach," Tristan called back.

"I'll be staying late tomorrow," the older man added, coming a few feet out of his office. "Maybe then you can pick up where you left off?"

Tristan looked at Ivy. She shrugged, then nodded, but kept her eyes down.

"Maybe," he said.

8

Ivy took a long route home that afternoon, driving a road that ran south from the center of Stonehill, following a tangle of shady streets lined with newer houses. She drove round and round, unwilling to make the final turn and head for the ridge. There was so much to think about. Why was Tristan doing this? Was he just feeling sorry for her? Did he want to be her friend? Did he want more than a friendship?

But it wasn't these questions that kept her driving. It was the luxury of remembering: how he had looked rising out of the water, a shimmer of drops spilling off him; how he had touched her, gently, so gently.

At home, she'd have to listen to her mother's story about the latest round of snobbery that

Maggie was encountering; she'd talk about the ups and downs of Philip's life as a third grader; she'd find a new way to say thanks for the things Andrew kept giving her, and walk on eggshells around Gregory. With all that going on, the moments of the afternoon would fade and be lost forever.

In her mind, Ivy saw Tristan in slow motion, swimming in a circle around her. She remembered the way his hands had felt when he helped her float, the way he had slowly tilted her head back in the water. She trembled with pleasure, and a little fear.

Angels, don't let go of me! she prayed.

This was something different from a crush. This was something that could flood out every other thought and feeling.

Maybe I should back out now, Ivy thought, before I'm in over my head. I'll call him tonight.

But then she remembered how he had pulled her through the water, his face full of light and laughter.

Ivy didn't see the car coming. Lost in thought, responding only to what was directly in front of her, she didn't see the dark car run the stop sign until the very last second. She slammed on her brakes. Both cars squealed and spun around, and for a moment were side by side, lightly touching. Then they veered away from each other. Letting her breath out slowly, Ivy sat still in the middle of the intersection.

The other driver threw open his door. A stream of four-letter words came rushing at her. Without even glancing in his direction, Ivy rolled up her window and checked her door locks. The shouting stopped suddenly. Ivy turned to look coolly at the driver.

"Gregory!"

She put her window down.

His skin was pale except for the scarlet that had crept up his cheeks. He stared at her, then glanced around the intersection, looking surprised, as if he were just now recognizing where he was and what had happened.

"Are you okay?" she asked.

"Yes . . . yes. Are you?"

"Well, I'm breathing again."

"I'm sorry," he said. "I—I wasn't paying attention, I guess. And I didn't know it was you, Ivy." Though his anger had subsided, he still looked upset.

"That's okay," she said. "I was driving in a daze, too."

He glanced through the window at the wet towel on her front seat.

"What are you doing around here?" he wanted to know.

She wondered if he would make the connection

between the wet towel and swimming and Tristan. But she hadn't even told Beth or Suzanne what she was doing. Besides, it wouldn't matter to Gregory.

"I needed to think about something. I know it sounds crazy, with all the space we have at the house, but I, well—"

"Needed other space," he finished for her. "I know how that is. Are you heading home now?"

"Yes."

"Follow me." He gave her a brief, lopsided smile. "Behind me, you'll be safer."

"You're sure you're okay?" she asked. His eyes still looked troubled.

He nodded, then returned to his car.

When they arrived home, Andrew pulled into the driveway after them.

He greeted Ivy, then turned to Gregory. "So how is your mother?"

Gregory shrugged. "Same as always."

"I'm glad you went to visit her today."

"I gave her your good wishes and fondest regards," Gregory said, his face and voice deadpan.

Andrew nodded and stepped around a spilled box of colored chalk. He bent over to look at what had once been clean, white concrete at the edge of his garage.

"Is anything new with her? Is there anything

I should know about?" he asked. He was studying the chalk drawings done by Philip; he didn't catch the pause, didn't see the emotion on Gregory's face that passed as fast as it came. But Ivy did.

"Nothing new," he said to his father.

"Good."

Ivy waited till the door closed behind Andrew.

"Do you want to talk about it?" she asked Gregory.

He spun around, as if he had forgotten that she was there.

"Talk about what?"

Ivy hesitated, then said, "You just told your father that everything's fine with your mom. But from the look on your face, at the intersection and just now, when you were talking about her, I thought maybe . . ."

Gregory played with his keys. "You're right. Things aren't fine. There may be some trouble ahead."

"With your mother?"

"I can't talk about it. Look, I appreciate your concern, but I can handle this myself. If you really want to help me, then don't say anything to anyone, all right? Don't even mention our little run-in. Promise me." His eyes held hers.

Ivy shrugged. "Promise," she said. "But if

you change your mind, you know where to find me."

"In the middle of an intersection," he said, giving her one of his wry smiles, then went inside.

Before going in, Ivy stopped to study Philip's concrete masterpiece. She recognized the bright aqua of her water angel, and the strong brown lines of Tony. After a moment, she identified the Mighty Morphin' Power Rangers. Philip's dragons were easy to spot; they usually looked as if they had swallowed a vat of lighter fluid, and they always fought the Power Rangers and angels. But what was that? A round head, with funny bits of hair and an orange stick coming out of each ear?

The name was scrawled on the side. Tristan.

Picking up a piece of black chalk, Ivy filled in two olive teeth. Now he looked like the guy who was kind enough to cheer up an eight-year-old having a very tough day. Ivy remembered the look on Tristan's face when she had yanked open the storeroom door. She threw back her head and laughed.

Back out now? Who was she kidding?

Tristan was sure he had scared Ivy away that first day, but she came back, and from the second lesson on he was very careful. He barely touched her; he coached her like a professional; and he kept dating what's her name and that other girl. But it was getting more difficult for him each day, being alone with Ivy, standing so close to her, hoping for some sign that she wanted something other than lessons and friendship.

"I think it's time, Ella," he said to the cat after two frustrating weeks of lessons. "She's not interested, and I can't stand it anymore. I'm going to get Ivy to sign up at the Y."

Ella purred.

"Then I'm going to find myself a monastery with a swim team."

The next day he made a conscious decision not to change into his bathing suit. He pocketed a brochure for the Y, strode out of the pool office, then stopped.

Ivy wasn't there. She forgot, he thought, then he saw Ivy's towel and ponytail holder down by the deep end. "Ivy!"

He ran to the edge of the pool and saw her in the twelve-foot section, lying all the way at the bottom, motionless. "Oh, my God!"

He dove straight off the side, pulling, pulling through the water to get to her. He yanked her up to the surface and swam for the pool's edge. It was difficult; she had come to and was struggling with him. His clothes were an extra, dragging weight. He heaved Ivy up on the side of the pool and sprang up beside her.

"What in the world—?" she said.

She wasn't coughing, wasn't sputtering, wasn't out of breath. She was just staring at him, at his soaked shirt, his clinging jeans, his sagging socks. Tristan stared back, then threw his waterlogged shoes as far as he could, down several rows of bleachers.

"What were you doing?" she asked.

"What were *you* doing?"

She opened her hand to show him a shiny copper penny. "Diving for this."

Anger surged through him. "The first rule of swimming, Ivy, is never, *never* swim alone!"

"But I had to do it, Tristan! I had to see if I could face my nightmare without you, without my—my lifeguard close by. And I could. I did," she said, a dazzling smile breaking over her face. Her hair was hanging loose around her shoulders. Her eyes were smiling into his, the color of an emerald sea in brilliant sunlight.

Then she blinked. "Is that what you were doing—being a lifeguard, being a hero?"

"No, Ivy," he said quietly, and stood up. "I was proving once again that I'm a hero to everyone but you."

"Wait a minute," she said, but he started to walk away.

"Wait a minute!" He didn't get far, not with the weight of her hanging on to one leg.

"I said *wait.*"

He tried to pull away, but she had him firmly anchored.

"Is that what you want, for me to say you're a hero?"

He grimaced. "I guess not. I guess I thought it would get me what I want. But it didn't."

"Well, what do you want?" she asked.

Was there any point in telling her now?

"To change into dry clothes," he said. "I've got some sweats in my locker."

"Okay." She released his leg. But before he could move away, she caught his hand. She held it in both of her hands for a moment, then lightly kissed the tips of his fingers.

She peeked up at him, gave a little shrug, then let go. But now it was he who held on, twining his fingers in hers. After a moment of hesitation, she rested her head against his hand. Could she feel it—the way just her lightest touch made his pulse race? He knelt down. Taking her other hand in his, he kissed her fingertips, then he laid his cheek in her palm.

She lifted up his face.

"Ivy," he said. The word was like a kiss. "Ivy."

The word became a kiss.

9

"He beat me!" Tristan said. "Philip beat me two out of three games!"

Ivy rested her hands on the piano keys, looked over her shoulder at Tristan, and laughed. It had been a week since their first trembling kiss. Every night she had fallen asleep dreaming about that kiss, and each kiss after.

It was all so incredible to her. She was aware of the lightest touch, the softest brush against him. Every time he called her name, her answer came from somewhere deep inside her. Yet there was something so easy and natural about being with him. Sometimes it felt as if Tristan had been a part of her life for years, sprawled as he was now on the floor of her music room, playing checkers with Philip.

"I can't believe he beat me two out of three!"

"Almost three out of three," Philip crowed.

"That will teach you not to mess with Ginger," Ivy said.

Tristan frowned down at the angel statue that stood alone on the checkerboard. Philip always used her as one of his playing pieces.

The three-inch china angel had once been Ivy's, but when Philip was in kindergarten, he'd decided to pretty her up. Pink-frost nail polish on her dress and crusty gold glitter on her hair had given her a whole new look; and Ivy had given her to Philip.

"Ginger's very smart," he told Tristan.

Tristan glanced up doubtfully at Ivy.

"Maybe next time Philip will let you borrow her and *you* can win," Ivy said with a smile, then turned to Philip. "Isn't it getting late?"

"Why do you always say that?" her brother asked.

Tristan grinned. "Because she's trying to get rid of you. Come on. We'll read two stories, like the last time, then it's lights out."

He walked Philip down to his bedroom. Ivy stayed upstairs and began to flip through her piano books, looking for songs that Tristan might like. He was into hard rock, but she couldn't exactly play it on the piano. He knew nothing about Beethoven and Bach. Tristan's idea of classical music was the musicals from his parents' collection. She ran through several songs from *Carousel,* then put the old book aside.

All night there had been music running through her like a silver river. Now she turned out the lights and played it from memory, Beethoven's *Moonlight Sonata.*

Tristan returned in the middle of the sonata. He saw the slight hesitation in her hands and heard the pause in the music.

"Don't stop," he said softly, and came to stand behind her.

Ivy played to the end. For a few moments after the last chord, neither of them spoke, neither of them moved. There was only the still, silver moonlight on the piano keys, and the music, the way music can linger on sometimes in silence.

Then Ivy rested her back against him.

"You want to dance?" Tristan asked.

Ivy laughed, and he pulled her up and they danced a circle around the room. She laid her head on his shoulder and felt his strong arms around her. They danced slow, slower. She wished he would never let go.

"How do you do that?" he whispered. "How do you dance with me and play the piano at the same time?"

"At the same time?" she asked.

"Isn't that *you* making the music I hear?"

Ivy pulled her head up. "Tristan, that line is so . . . so . . ."

"Corny," he said. "But it got you to look up at me." Then he swiftly lowered his mouth and stole a long, soft kiss.

"Don't forget to tell Tristan to stop by the shop sometime," Lillian said. "Betty and I would love to see him again. We're very fond of chunks."

"*Hunks,* Lillian," Ivy said with a grin. "Tristan is a hunk." My hunk, she thought, then picked up a box wrapped in brown paper. "Is this everything to be delivered?"

"Yes, thank you, dear. I know it's out of your way."

"Not too far," Ivy said, starting out the door.

"Five-twenty-eight Willow Street," Betty called from the back of the store.

"Five-thirty," Lillian said quietly.

Well, that narrows it down, Ivy thought, passing through the door of 'Tis the Season. She glanced at her watch. Now she wouldn't have time to spend with her friends.

Suzanne and Beth had been waiting for her at the mall's food court.

"You said you would be off twenty minutes ago," Suzanne complained.

"I know. It's been one of those days," Ivy replied. "Will you walk me to my car? I have to deliver this, then get right home."

"Did you hear that? She has to get right home," Suzanne said to Beth, "for a birthday party, that's what she *says*. She *says* it's Philip's ninth birthday."

"It's May twenty-eighth," Ivy responded. "You know it is, Suzanne."

"But for all we know," Suzanne went on to Beth, "it's a private wedding on the hill."

Ivy rolled her eyes, and Beth laughed. Suzanne still hadn't forgiven her for keeping secret the swimming lessons.

"Is Tristan coming tonight?" Beth asked as they exited the mall.

"He's one of Philip's two guests," Ivy replied, "and will be sitting next to Philip, not me, and playing all night with Philip, not me. Tristan promised. It was about the only way to keep my brother from coming with us to the prom. Hey, where did you two park?"

Suzanne couldn't remember and Beth hadn't noticed. Ivy drove them around and around the mall lot. Beth looked for the car while Suzanne advised Ivy on clothes and romance. She covered everything from telephone strategies and how not to be too available to working hard at looking casual. She had been giving volumes of advice for the last three weeks.

"Suzanne, I think you make dating too complicated," Ivy said at last. "All this plotting and planning. It seems pretty simple to me."

Incredibly simple, she thought. Whether she and Tristan were relaxing or studying together, whether they were sitting silently side by side or both trying to talk at the same time—which they did frequently—these last few weeks had been incredibly easy.

"That's because he's the one," Beth said knowingly.

There was only one thing about Ivy that Tristan couldn't understand. The angels.

"You've had a difficult life," he had said to her one night. It was the night of the prom—or rather, the morning after, but not yet dawn. They were walking barefoot in the grass, away from the house to the far edge of the ridge. In the west, a crescent moon hung like a leftover Christmas ornament. There was one star. Far below them, a train wound its silver path through the valley.

"You've been through so much, I don't blame you for believing," Tristan said.

"You don't blame me? You don't *blame* me? What do you mean by that?" But she knew what he meant. To him, an angel was just a pretty teddy bear—something for a child to cling to.

He held her tightly in his arms. "I can't believe, Ivy. I have all I need and all I want right here on earth," he said. "Right *here*. In my arms."

"Well, I don't," she replied, and even in the pale light, she could see the sting in his eyes. They started to fight then. Ivy realized for the first time that the more you love, the more you hurt. What was worse, you hurt for him as well as for yourself.

After he left, she cried all morning. Her phone calls hadn't been returned that afternoon. But he came back in the evening, with fifteen lavender roses. One for each angel, he said.

"Ivy! Ivy, did you hear anything I just said?" Suzanne asked, jolting her back to the present. "You know, I thought if we got you a boyfriend, you'd come down to earth a little. But I was wrong. Head still in the clouds! Angel zone!"

"*We* didn't get her a boyfriend," Beth said quietly but firmly. "They found each other. Here's the car, Ivy. Have a good time tonight. We'd better dash, it's going to storm."

The girls jumped out and Ivy checked her watch again. Now she was really late. She sped over the access road and down the highway.

When she crossed the river, she noticed how rapidly the dark clouds were moving.

Her delivery was to one of the newer houses south of town, the same neighborhood where she had driven after her first swimming lesson with Tristan. It seemed as if everything she did now made her think of him.

She got just as lost this time, driving around in circles, with one eye on the clouds. Thunder rumbled. The trees shivered and turned over their leaves, shining an eerie lime green against the leaden sky. The wind began to gust. Branches whipped, and blossoms and tender leaves were torn too soon from their limbs. Ivy leaned forward in her seat, intent on finding the right house before the storm broke.

Just finding the right street was difficult. She thought she was on Willow, but the sign said Fernway, with Willow running into it. She got out of her car to see if the sign could have been turned—a popular sport among kids in town. Then she heard a loud motor making the bend on the hill above her. She stepped out into the street to wave down the motorcyclist. For a moment, the Harley slowed, then the engine was gunned and the cyclist flew past her.

Well, she'd have to go with her instincts. The lawns were steep there, and Lillian had said that Mrs. Abromaitis lived on a hill, a flight of stone steps lined with flowerpots leading up to her house.

Ivy drove around the bend. She could feel the rising wind rocking her car. Overhead the pale sky was being swallowed up by inky clouds.

Ivy screeched to a halt in front of two houses and pulled the box out of the car, struggling with it against the wind. Both houses had stone steps that ran up side by side. Both had flowerpots. She chose one set of steps, and just as she cleared the first flowerpot it blew over and crashed behind her. Ivy screamed, then laughed at herself.

At the top of the steps she looked at one house, then the other, 528 and 530, hoping for some kind of clue. A car was pulled around the back of 528, hidden by bushes, so someone was probably home. Then she saw a figure in the large window of 528—someone looking out for her, she thought, though she couldn't tell if it was a man or a woman, or if the person actually beckoned to her. All she could see was a vague shape of a person as part of the window's reflected collage of thrashing trees backlit by flashes of lightning. She started toward the house. The figure disappeared. At the same time, the front porch light went on at 530. The screen door banged back in the wind.

"Ivy? Ivy?" A woman called to her from the lit porch.

"Whew!" She made a run for it, handed off the package, and raced for her car. The skies opened, throwing down ropes of rain. Well, it wouldn't be the first time Tristan had seen her looking like a drowned rat.

Ivy, Gregory, and Andrew arrived home late, and Maggie looked miffed. Philip, of course, didn't care. He, Tristan, and his new school pal, Sammy, were playing a video game, one of the many gifts Andrew had bought for his birthday.

Tristan grinned up at the drenched Ivy. "I'm glad I taught you to swim," he said, then got up to kiss her.

She was dripping all over the hardwood floor. "I'll soak you," she warned.

He wrapped his arms around her and pulled her close. "I'll dry," he whispered. "Besides, it's fun to gross out Philip."

"Ew," said Philip, as if on cue.

"Mush," agreed Sammy.

Ivy and Tristan held on to each other and laughed. Then Ivy ran upstairs to change her clothes and wring out her hair. She put on lipstick, no other makeup—her eyes were already bright and her cheeks full of color. She

117

scrounged around in her jewelry box for a pair of earrings, then hurried downstairs just in time to see Philip finish opening his presents.

"She's wearing her peacock ears tonight," Philip told Tristan as Ivy sat down to dinner across from the two of them.

"Darn," said Tristan, "I forgot to put in my carrot sticks."

"And your shrimp tails." Philip snickered.

Ivy wondered who was happier at that moment, Philip or her. She knew that life did not seem so good to Gregory. It had been a rough week for him; he had confided in her that he was still very worried about his mother, though he wouldn't tell her why. Lately his father and he had had little to say to each other. Maggie struggled to converse with him but usually gave up.

Ivy turned to him now. "The tickets to the Yankee game were a terrific idea. Philip was thrilled with the present."

"He had a funny way of showing it."

It was true. Philip had thanked him very politely, then leaped up with excitement when he saw the old *Sports Illustrated* spread on Don Mattingly that Tristan had dug up.

During dinner Ivy made an effort to keep Gregory in the conversation. Tristan tried to talk to him about sports and cars but received mostly one-word replies. Andrew looked irritated, though Tristan didn't seem to take offense.

Andrew's cook, Henry—who'd been let go after the wedding, but reinstated after six weeks of Maggie's cooking—had made them a delicious dinner. Maggie, however, had insisted on baking her son's birthday cake. Henry carried in the heavy, lopsided thing, his eyes averted.

Philip's face lit up. "It's Mistake Cake!"

The rich and lumpy chocolate frosting supported nine candles at various angles. Lights were quickly extinguished and everyone sang to Philip. With the last measure, the doorbell chimed. Andrew frowned and rose to answer it.

From her seat, Ivy could see into the hall. Two police officers, a man and a woman, talked with Andrew. Gregory leaned into Ivy to see what was going on.

"What do you think it's about?" Ivy whispered.

"Something at the college," he guessed.

Tristan looked across the table questioningly and Ivy shrugged her shoulders. Her mother, unaware that there might be something wrong, kept cutting the cake.

Then Andrew stepped back into the room.

"Maggie." She must have read something in

his eyes. She dropped the knife immediately and went to Andrew's side. He took her hand.

"Gregory and Ivy, would you join us in the library, please? Tristan, could you stay with the boys?" he asked.

The officers were still waiting in the hall. Andrew led the way to the library. If there were a problem at the college, we wouldn't be gathering like this, thought Ivy.

When everyone was seated, Andrew said, "There's no easy way to begin. Gregory, your mother has died."

"Oh, no," Maggie said softly.

Ivy turned quickly to Gregory. He sat stiffly, his eyes on his father, and said nothing.

"The police received an anonymous call about five-thirty P.M. that someone at her address needed help. When they arrived, they found her dead, a gunshot wound to her head."

Gregory didn't blink. Ivy reached out for his hand. It was cold as ice.

"The police have asked— They need— As a matter of normal procedure—" Andrew's voice wavered. He turned to face the police officers. "Perhaps one of you can take over from here?"

"As a matter of procedure," the woman officer said, "we need to ask a few questions. We are still searching the house for any information that might be relevant to the case, though it seems fairly conclusive that her death was a suicide."

"Oh, God!" said Maggie.

"What evidence do you have for that?" Gregory asked. "While it's true my mother was depressed, she has been since the beginning of April—"

"Oh, God!" Maggie said again. Andrew reached out for her, but she moved away from him.

Ivy knew what her mother was thinking. She remembered the scene a week earlier, when a picture of Caroline and Andrew had somehow turned up in the hall desk. Andrew had told Maggie to throw it in the trash. Maggie could not. She didn't want to think that she was the one who had "thrown Caroline out" of her home—years earlier, or now. Ivy guessed that her mother felt responsible for Caroline's unhappiness, and now her death.

"I'd still like to know," Gregory continued, "what makes you think that she killed herself. That doesn't seem like her. It doesn't seem like her at all. She was too strong a woman."

Ivy could hardly believe how clearly and steadily Gregory could speak.

"First, there is circumstantial evidence," said the policeman. "No actual note, but photographs

that were torn and scattered around the body."
He glanced toward Maggie.

"Photographs of . . . ?" Gregory asked.

Andrew sucked in his breath.

"Mr. and Mrs. Baines," said the officer.
"Newspaper photos from their wedding."

Andrew watched helplessly as Maggie bent
over in her chair, her head down, wrapping her
arms around her knees.

Ivy let go of Gregory's hand, wanting to
comfort her mother, but he pulled her back.

"The gun was still twisted around her
thumb. There were powder burns on her fingers, the burns one gets from firing such a
weapon. Of course, we'll be checking the gun
for prints and the bullet for a match, and we'll
let you know if we find something unexpected.
But her doors were locked—no sign of forced
entry—her air-conditioning on and windows se-
cure, so . . ."

Gregory took a deep breath. "So I guess she
wasn't as tough as I thought. What—what time
do you think this happened?"

"Between five and five-thirty P.M., not that
long before we got there."

An eerie feeling washed over Ivy. She had
been driving through the neighborhood then.
She had been watching the angry sky and the
trees lashing themselves. Had she driven by

Caroline's house? Had Caroline killed herself in the fury of the storm?

Andrew asked if he could talk later with the police and guided Maggie out of the room. Gregory stayed behind to answer questions about his mother and any relationships or problems he knew about. Ivy wanted to leave; she didn't want to hear the details of Caroline's life and longed to be with Tristan, longed for his steadying arms around her.

But Gregory again held her back. His hand was cold and unresponsive to hers and his face still expressionless. His voice was so calm she found it spooky. But something inside him was struggling, some small part of him admitted the horror of what had just happened, and asked for her. So she stayed with him, long after Tristan had gone and everyone else was in bed.

10

"But you told me Gary wanted to go out *Friday* night," Ivy said.

"He did," Tristan replied, lying back next to her in the grass. "But his date changed her mind. I think she got a better offer."

Ivy shook her head. "Why does Gary always chase the golden girls?"

"Why does Suzanne chase Gregory?" he countered.

Ivy smiled. "Same reason Ella chases butterflies, I guess." She watched the cat's leaping ballet. Ella was very much at home in Reverend Carruthers's garden. In the midst of snapdragons, lilies, roses, and herbs, Tristan's father had planted a little patch of catnip.

"Is Saturday night a problem?" Tristan asked.

"If you're working, we could make it a late movie."

Ivy sat up. Tristan came first with her, always. But with their plans set for Friday night and Sunday too—well, she might as well blurt it out, she thought. "Gregory has invited Suzanne, Beth, and me out with some of his friends that night."

Tristan didn't hide his surprise or his displeasure.

"Suzanne was so eager," Ivy said quickly. "And Beth was really excited, too—she doesn't go out very much."

"And you?" Tristan asked, propping himself up on one elbow, twisting a long piece of grass.

"I think I should go—for Gregory's sake."

"You've been doing a lot for Gregory's sake in the last few weeks."

"Tristan, his mother killed herself!" Ivy exploded.

"I know that."

"I live in the same house with him," she went on. "I share the same kitchen and hallways and family room. I see his moods, his ups and downs. Lots of downs," she added softly, thinking about how some days Gregory did nothing but sit and read the newspaper, thumbing through it as if in search of something, but never finding it.

"I think he's very angry," she went on. "He tries to hide it, but I think he's furious at his mother for killing herself. The other night, one-thirty in the morning, he was out on the tennis court, banging balls against the wall."

That night, Ivy had gone out to talk to him. When she had called to him, he turned, and she had seen the depth of his anger and his pain.

"Believe me, Tristan, I help him when I can, and I'll keep on helping him, but if you think I have any special feelings for him, if you think he and I— That's ridiculous! If you think— I can't believe you'd—"

"Whoa, whoa." He wrestled her down in the grass with him.

"I'm not worried about anything like that."

"Then what's bugging you?"

"Two things, I guess," he replied. "One, I think you may be doing a lot out of guilt."

"Guilt!" She pushed him back and sat up again.

"I think you've picked up your mother's attitude, that she and her family are responsible for Caroline's unhappiness."

"We're not."

"I know that. I just want to make sure you do—and that you're not trying to make it up to someone who is milking it for all it's worth."

"You don't know what you're talking about,"

Ivy said, pulling up tufts of grass. "You really don't know what he's going through. You haven't been around Gregory. You—"

"I've been around him since first grade."

"People can change from first grade."

"I've known Eric for that long, too," Tristan continued. "They've done some pretty wild, even dangerous things together. And that's the other thing that worries me."

"But Gregory wouldn't try stuff with my friends and me around," Ivy insisted. "He respects me, Tristan. This is just his way of reaching out, after the last three weeks."

Tristan didn't look convinced.

"Please don't let this come between us," she said.

He reached up for her face. "I wouldn't let anything come between us. Not mountains, rivers, continents, war, floods—"

"Or dire death itself," she said. "So you did read Beth's latest story."

"Gary ate it up."

"Gary? You're kidding!"

"He kept the copy you gave me," Tristan said, "but I swore to him that I'd tell you I lost it."

Ivy laughed and lay down close to Tristan, resting her head on his shoulder. "You understand, then, why I said yes to Gregory."

"No, but it's your choice," he said. "And that's that. So what are you doing *next* Saturday night?"

"What are *you* doing?" Ivy asked back.

"Dining at the Durney Inn."

"The inn! Well, we must be earning big bucks giving swimming lessons this summer."

"We're earning enough," he said. "You don't happen to know of a beautiful girl who likes to be treated to candlelight and French food, do you?"

"Yeah, I do."

"Is she free that night?"

"Maybe. Does she get an appetizer?"

"Three, if she likes."

"How about dessert?"

"Raspberry soufflé. And kisses."

"*Kisses . . .*"

"Well, that was fun," Ivy remarked dryly.

"I was bored anyway," Eric said.

"I wasn't," Beth told them. She was the last one to leave the party at the campus sorority house that Saturday night. Borrowing paper from one of the sorority sisters, she had interviewed just about everyone there. When the other high-schoolers had been thrown out, she was invited to stay. Sigma Pi Nu was flattered that she would put them in a story.

"Eric, you're going to have to learn to keep

your cool," Gregory said, clearly irritated. He had been in the corner with some redhead (which had prompted Suzanne to go body to body with a bearded guy) when Eric decided to pick a fight with a giant wearing a varsity football shirt. Not smart.

Now Eric stood on the steps of a pillared building, staring up at a statue and cocking his head left and right, as if he were conversing with it.

Suzanne lay on her back on a stone bench in the college quad, laughing softly to herself, her bare knees up, her skirt fluttering back provocatively. Gregory eyed her.

Ivy turned away. She and Will were the only ones who hadn't been drinking. Will had seemed at home at the campus party scene, but restless. Perhaps the rumors at school were true: he had seen it all and nothing much impressed him.

Like Ivy, Will had been a newcomer in January. His father was a television producer in New York, however, which scored big points with the kids at school. Upon arrival, he had been immediately taken up by the fast crowd, but his silent manner kept everyone from getting a real fix on him. It was easy to imagine a lot of things about Will, and most people that Ivy knew imagined he was very cool.

"Where'sss your old man?" Eric suddenly

shouted. He was still peering up at the statue on the steps. "G.B., where's your old man?"

"That's my old man's old man," Gregory replied.

Ivy realized then that it was a statue of Gregory's grandfather. Of course. They were in front of Baines Hall.

"Why isssn't your old man up there?"

Gregory sat down on a bench across from Suzanne. "I guess because he's not dead yet." He took a deep swig from a beer bottle.

"Then why isssn't your old lady up there? Huh?"

Gregory didn't reply. He took another long drink.

Eric frowned up at the statue. "I miss her. I misssss old Caroline. You know I do."

"I know," Gregory said quietly.

"Ssso, let's put her up there." He winked at Gregory.

Gregory didn't say anything, and Ivy went to stand behind him. She rested one hand lightly on Gregory's shoulder.

"I got Caroline right here in my pocket," Eric said.

All of them watched as he patted and searched his shirt and pants. Finally he pulled out a bra. He held it up to his cheek. "Still warm."

Ivy laid her other hand on Gregory's shoulder. She could feel the tension in him.

Eric wrapped the bra around his arm and struggled to climb up on the statue.

"You're going to kill yourself," Gregory told him.

"Like your mother," said Eric.

Gregory made no response except to take another drink. Ivy turned his head away from Eric. Gregory let his face rest against her then, and she felt him relax a little. Both Suzanne and Will watched the two of them, Suzanne with flashing eyes.

But Ivy stayed where she was while Eric put the bra on Judge Baines. Then she confiscated a few unopened beers and walked over to Suzanne. "Gregory could use some hand-holding," she said to her friend.

"Even after you and the redhead."

Ivy ignored the comment. Suzanne also had had too much to drink.

Eric gave a sudden yelp, and they turned quickly to see him sliding off the statue. He landed in the gravel and rolled up like a snail. Will hurried over to him. Gregory laughed.

"Nothing broken but my brain," Eric muttered as Will pulled him to his feet.

"I think we should get back to the car," Will said coolly.

"But the party's just begun," Gregory protested, rising to his feet. The alcohol was obviously kicking in. "I haven't felt this good since who knows when."

"I know when," said Eric.

"The party will be over soon enough if the campus police catch us," Will pointed out.

"My father's the prez," said Gregory. "He'll get us off the hook."

"Or hang us from a higher one," said Eric.

Ivy looked at her watch: 11:45. She wondered where Tristan was and what he was doing. She wondered if he missed her. She could have been sitting next to him at that moment, enjoying the soft June night.

"Come on, Beth," she said, sorry she had gotten her friends into this situation. "Suzanne," she commanded.

"Yes, *mother*," Suzanne replied.

Gregory laughed, which stung Ivy a little. They're both wasted, she reminded herself.

It took a long time for the six of them to find Gregory's car again. When they did, Will held out his hand for Gregory's keys. "How about if I drive?"

"I can handle it," Gregory told him.

"Not this time." Will's tone was easygoing, but he reached determinedly for the keys.

Gregory yanked them away. "Nobody drives this Beamer but me."

Will glanced over at Ivy.

"Come on, Gregory," she said. "Let me be the D.D."

"If someone else drives," Will pointed out to Gregory, "you can drink all you want."

"I'll drink all I want *and* I'll drive all I want," Gregory shouted, "and if you don't like it, walk."

Ivy thought about walking—to the nearest phone and calling for a ride. But she knew Suzanne would stay with Gregory, and she felt responsible for her safety.

Will asked Ivy if he could borrow her sweater, then stuffed that and his jacket between the two front seats, making a seat in the middle. He pulled Eric into the front of the car with him, so that Gregory, he, and Eric sat three across. Ivy climbed into the middle of the backseat, with Beth and Suzanne on either side.

"Why, Will," Gregory said, observing the way he was squeezed in next to him, "I didn't know you cared. Suzanne, get up here!"

Ivy pulled Suzanne back.

"I said, get up here. Let Will sit back there with the girl of his dreams."

Ivy shook her head and sighed.

"Anybody likely to throw up has to sit by a window," Will said.

Ivy buckled Suzanne's seat belt.

Gregory shrugged, then started the car. He drove fast, too fast. The tires squealed on turns, the rubber barely holding the road. Beth closed her eyes. Suzanne and Eric hung their heads out the window as the car lurched sickeningly from side to side. Ivy stared straight ahead, her muscles contracting each time Gregory had to brake or turn the car, as if she were driving the route for him. Will actually did help drive. Ivy realized then why he had placed himself in a dangerous spot without a seat belt.

They were snaking south on the back roads, and when they finally crossed the river into town, Ivy let out a sigh of relief. But Gregory made a sharp turn north again, taking the road that ran along the river and beneath the ridge, past the train depot, beyond town limits.

"Where are we going?" Ivy asked as they followed a narrow road, their headlights striping the trees.

"You'll see."

Eric lifted his head off the door. "Chick, chick, chick," he sang. "Who's a chick, chick, chick?"

The ridge, looming high and dark on their

right, crowded the road closer and closer to the train tracks on the left. Ivy knew they must be getting near to the point where the tracks crossed over the river.

"The double bridges," Beth whispered to her, just as they ran out of road. Gregory cut the engine and lights. Ivy couldn't see a thing.

"Who's a chick chick chick?" Eric said, swinging his head back and forth.

Ivy felt ill from the fumes of the car and the alcohol. She and Beth climbed out of one side. Suzanne sat with the door open on the other. Gregory popped open the trunk. More beer.

"Where did you get all this?" Ivy demanded.

Gregory grinned and put a heavy arm around her. "Something else for you to thank Andrew for."

"Andrew bought it?" she said incredulously.

"No, his credit card did."

Then he and Eric each reached for a six-pack.

Though Ivy understood Gregory's need to blow off steam, though she knew how tough it had been for him since his mother's death, she had been growing angrier by the minute. Now her anger began to ebb, giving way to a slow tide of fear.

The river wasn't far away; she could hear it rushing over rocks. As her eyes adjusted to the country dark she traced the high wires of the electric train line. She remembered why kids came here: to play chicken on the railroad bridge. Ivy didn't want to follow Gregory as he led them single file to the bridges. But she couldn't stay behind, not with Suzanne unable to take care of herself.

Eric was pushing her from behind, singing in a high, weird voice, "Who's a chick, chick, chick?"

Small round stones rolled under their feet. Eric and Suzanne kept tripping on the railroad ties. The six of them walked the avenue that sliced sharply through the trees, a path made by the trains rushing between New York City and towns north of it.

The avenue opened out and Ivy saw the two bridges side by side, the new one built about seven feet from the old. Two gleaming steel rails penciled the path of the new one. There was no railing or restraining fence. The fretwork beneath it stretched like a dark and sinister web across the river. The older bridge had collapsed in the middle. Each side was like a hand extending from the river banks, fingers of metal and rotting wood reaching toward but unable to grip the others.

Far below both bridges, the water rushed and hissed.

"Follow the leader, follow the leader," Eric said, prancing ahead of them. He stumbled toward the newer bridge.

Ivy looped two fingers through the waistband of Suzanne's skirt. "Not you."

"Let go of me," Suzanne snapped.

Suzanne tried to follow Eric onto the bridge, but Ivy pulled her back.

"Let go!"

They struggled for a moment, and Gregory laughed at the two of them. Then Suzanne slipped out of Ivy's grasp. Desperate, Ivy reached forward and caught Suzanne's bare leg, causing her to trip over the rail and tumble down the track's bed of stone into some brush. Suzanne tried to pull herself up but couldn't. She sank back, her eyes blazing at Ivy, her hands curled with anger.

"Beth, you'd better see if she's all right," Ivy said, and turned her attention back to Eric. He was fifteen feet out now and over the water. His too-thin body skipped and turned along the track like a dancing skeleton.

"Chick, chick, chicken," he taunted the others. "Look at all you chick, chick, chickens."

Gregory leaned against a tree and laughed. Will watched, his expression guarded.

Then everyone's head turned as the whistle sounded from across the river.

It was the whistle of the late-night train that Ivy had heard so often from their house high on the ridge, a streamer of sound that wrapped around her heart every night as if it wanted to take her with it.

"Eric!" she and Will shouted at the same time. Beth held Suzanne, who was leaning over the bushes and throwing up.

"Eric!"

Will started after him, but Eric took off, crazily bobbing over the tracks. Will pursued.

They'll both be killed, thought Ivy. "Will, come back! Will! You can't!"

The train made its swing onto the bridge, its bright eye throwing back the night, burning the two boys into paper-thin silhouettes. Ivy saw Eric tottering on the very edge of the bridge. Water and rocks lay far below him.

He's going to jump to the old bridge, she thought. He'll never make it.

Angels, help us! she prayed. Water angel, where are you? Tony? I'm calling you!

Eric leaned down, then suddenly dropped over the side.

Ivy screamed. She and Beth screamed and screamed.

138

Will was running back now, stumbling and running. The train wasn't slowing down. It was huge and dark. It was as large as night itself, bearing down on him behind one bright, blind eye. Twenty feet, fifteen feet— Will wasn't going to make it! He looked like a moth being drawn into its light.

"Will! Will!" Ivy shrieked. "Oh, angels—"

He leaped.

The train rushed by, the ground thundering beneath it, the air burning with metal smells. Ivy took off down the steep hill, crashing through the brush in the direction that Will had leaped.

"Will? Will, answer me!"

"I'm here. I'm okay."

He stood up in front of her.

By the hands of the angels, she thought.

They held on to each other for a moment. Ivy didn't know if it was he or she who was shaking so violently.

"Eric? Did he—"

"I don't know," she answered quickly. "Can we get down to the river from here?"

"Try the other side."

They clawed their way up the bank together. When they got to the top, they both stopped and stared. Eric was walking toward them along the new bridge, a thick rope and a bungee cord slung casually over his shoulder.

It took them a moment to figure out what had occurred. Ivy spun around to look at Gregory. Had he been in on the trick?

He was smiling now. "Excellent," he said to Eric. "Excellent."

11

"You know what I don't understand?" Gregory said, cocking his head, studying Ivy in her short silk skirt. A mischievous smile spread over his face. "I don't understand why you never wear that nice bridesmaid's dress."

Maggie looked up from the plate of snacks she was carrying upstairs to Andrew. Everyone was going out that evening.

"Oh, it's much too formal for the Durney Inn," Maggie said, "but you're right, Gregory, Ivy should find someplace to wear her dress again."

Ivy smiled briefly at her mother, then shot Gregory a wicked look. He grinned at her.

After Maggie had left the kitchen, he said, "You look hot tonight." He said it in a matter-of-fact way, though his eyes lingered on her. Ivy no longer tried to figure out what Gregory meant by some of his comments—whether he was truly giving a compliment or subtly mocking her. She let a lot of what he said roll right on by. Maybe she had finally gotten used to him.

"You're getting used to making excuses for him," Tristan had said after she told him what had happened on Saturday night.

Ivy had been furious at Eric for his stupid trick. Gregory wouldn't admit to being in on the stunt. He had shrugged and said, "You never know what Eric's up to. That's what makes him fun."

Of course, she had been angry at Gregory too. But living with him day after day, she saw how he struggled. Since his mother's death there were hours when he seemed completely lost in his own thoughts. She thought about the day he had asked her to go for a ride and they had driven through his mother's old neighborhood. She had told him that she had been there that stormy night. He had barely spoken after that and wouldn't meet her eyes the rest of the way home.

"I'd have to be a stone not to feel for him," Ivy had told Tristan, and ended the discussion there.

Both Gregory and Tristan were inclined to avoid each other. As usual, Gregory disappeared as soon as Tristan drove up that evening.

Tristan always came early to play for a few minutes with Philip. Ivy saw, with some satisfaction, that this time Tristan couldn't concentrate, though the home team was down by two in the rubber match of the series with Don Mattingly coming to bat. Second base was stolen while the pitcher was sneaking peeks at Ivy.

Philip grew frustrated the third time that Tristan couldn't remember how many outs there were, and stomped off to call Sammy. Ivy and Tristan seized the opportunity to slip out of the house. On the way to the car, Ivy noticed that Tristan seemed unusually quiet.

"How's Ella?" she asked.

"Good."

Ivy waited. Usually he told her a funny Ella story. "Just good?"

"Very good."

"Did you get a new bell for her collar?"

"Yes."

"Is something wrong, Tristan?"

He didn't answer right away. It's Gregory, she thought. He still has himself all wound up about Gregory and last weekend.

"Tell me!"

He faced her. With one finger he touched the back of her neck. Her hair was pinned up that night. Her shoulders were bare, except for two thin little straps. The top she wore was a simple camisole, with small buttons down the front.

Tristan ran his hand down her neck, then across her bare shoulder. "Sometimes it's hard to believe you're real," he said.

Ivy swallowed. Ever so gently he kissed her throat.

"Maybe . . . maybe we should get in the car," she suggested, glancing up at the windows of the house.

"Right."

He opened the door. There were roses on the seat, more lavender roses. "Whoops, I forgot," said Tristan. "Do you want to run them back inside?"

She picked them up and held them close to her face. "I want them with me."

"They'll probably wilt," he told her.

"We can stick them in a water glass at the restaurant."

Tristan smiled. "That will show the maître d' what kind of class we have."

"They're beautiful!"

"Yeah," he said softly. His eyes ran all over her, as if he were memorizing her. Then he kissed her on the forehead and held the roses while she got in the car.

As they drove they talked about their plans for the summer. Ivy was glad Tristan took the old routes rather than the highway. The trees were cool and musky with June. Light dappled their branches like gold coins slipping through angels' fingers. Tristan drove the winding roads with one hand on the steering wheel, the other reaching out for hers, as if she might slip away.

"I want to go to Juniper Lake," Ivy said. "I'm going to float out there in the deepest part, float for an hour, with the sun shooting sparkles at my fingers and toes—"

"Till along comes a big fish," Tristan teased.

"I'll float in the moonlight too," she went on.

"The moonlight? You'd swim in the dark?"

"With you I would. We could skinny-dip."

He glanced over at her and their eyes held for a moment.

"Better not look at you and drive at the same time," he said.

"Then stop driving," she replied quietly.

He glanced quickly at her, and she put her hand over her mouth. The words had escaped, and she suddenly felt shy and embarrassed. Couples dressed up and on their way to expensive restaurants didn't pull over to make out.

"We'll be late for our reservation," she said. "You should keep going."

Tristan eased the car off the road.

"There's the river," he said. "Do you want to walk down to it?"

"Yes."

She laid the roses in the back of the car. Tristan came around to open Ivy's door

"Are you going to be able to walk in those shoes?" Tristan asked, glancing down at Ivy's high heels.

She stood up. Both heels sank straight down in the mud.

Ivy laughed, and Tristan picked her up. "I'll give you a lift," he said.

"No, you'll drop me in the mud!"

"Not till we get there," he said, and hoisted her up higher till he held her legs, letting the top half of her fall over his shoulder as if he were carrying a sack.

Ivy laughed and pounded him on the back. Her hair was coming out of its pins. "My hair! My hair! Let me down!"

He pulled her back, and she slid down the front of him, her skirt riding up, her hair tumbling down.

"Ivy."

He held her so tightly against him, she could feel the trembling up and down his body.

"Ivy?" he whispered.

She opened her mouth and pressed it against his neck.

At the same time, they both reached for the handle and pulled open the car's back door.

"I never knew how romantic a backseat could be," Ivy joked a while later. She rested against the seat, smiling at Tristan. Then she looked past him at the pile of junk on the car floor. "Maybe you should pull your tie out of that old Burger King cup."

Tristan reached down and grimaced. He tossed the dripping thing into the front of the car, then sat back next to Ivy.

"Ow!" The smell of crushed flowers filled the air.

Ivy laughed out loud.

"What's so funny?" Tristan asked, pulling from behind him the smashed roses, but he was laughing, too.

"What if someone had come along and seen your father's Clergy sticker on the bumper?"

Tristan tossed the flowers in the front seat and pulled her toward him again. He traced the silk strap of her dress, then tenderly kissed her shoulder. "I'd have told then I was with an angel."

"Oh, what a line!"

"Ivy, I love you!" Tristan said, his face suddenly serious.

She stared back at him, then bit her lip. "This isn't some kind of game for me. I love you, Ivy, and one day you're going to believe me."

She put her arms around him and held him tightly. "Love *you*," she whispered into his neck. Ivy did believe him, and she trusted him as she trusted no one else. One day she'd have the nerve to say it, all of the words out loud. I love you, Tristan. She'd shout it out the windows. She'd string a banner straight across the school pool.

It took a few minutes to straighten themselves up. Ivy started laughing again. Tristan smiled and watched her try to tame her gold tumbleweed of hair—a useless effort. Then he started the car, urging it over the ruts and stones and onto the narrow road.

"Last glimpse of the river," he said as the road made a sharp turn away from it.

The June sun, dropping over the west ridge of the Connecticut countryside, shafted light on the very tops of the trees, flaking them with gold. The winding road slipped below, into a tunnel of maples, poplars, and oaks. Ivy felt as if she were sliding under the waves with Tristan, the setting sun glittering on top, the two of them moving together through a chasm of blue, purple, and deep green. Tristan flicked on his headlights.

"You really don't have to hurry," said Ivy. "I'm not hungry anymore."

"I ruined your appetite?"

She shook her head. "I guess I'm all filled up with happiness," she said softly.

The car sped along and took a curve sharply.

"I said, we don't have to hurry."

"That's funny," Tristan murmured. "I wonder what's—" He glanced down at his feet. "This doesn't feel . . ."

"Slow down, okay? It doesn't matter if we're a little late— Oh!" Ivy pointed straight ahead. "Tristan!"

Something had plunged through the bushes and into the roadway. She hadn't seen what it was, just the flicker of motion among the deep shadows. Then the deer stopped. It turned its head, its eyes drawn to the car's bright headlights.

"Tristan!"

They were rushing toward the shining eyes.

"Tristan, don't you see it?"

Rushing still.

"Ivy, something's—"

"A deer!" she exclaimed.

The animal's eyes blazed. Then light came from behind it, a bright burst around its dark shape. A car was coming from the opposite direction. Trees walled them in. There was no room to veer left or right.

"Stop!" she shouted.

"I'm—"

"Stop, why don't you stop?" she pleaded. "Tristan, *stop!*"

12

It was dazzling: the eye of the deer like a dark tunnel, the center of it bursting with light. Tristan braked and braked, but nothing would stop the rushing, nothing could keep him from speeding through the long funnel of darkness into an explosion of light.

For a moment he felt a tremendous weight, as if the trees and sky had collapsed on him. Then, with the explosion of light, the weight was lifted. Somehow he had gotten free.

She needs you.

"Ivy!" he called out.

The darkness swirled in again, the road around him like a Twirl-a-paint, black spinning with red, night swirling with the pulsing light of an ambulance.

She needs you.

He did not hear it, but he understood it. Did the others? "Ivy! Where's Ivy? You have to help Ivy!"

She was lying still. Bathed in red.

"Somebody help her! You've got to save her!"

But he could not hold on to the paramedic, could not even pull on his sleeve.

"No pulse," a woman said. "No chance."

"Help her!"

The swirling ran long and streaky now. Ribbons of light and dark rushed past him horizontally. Was she with him? The siren wailed: *I-veee. I-veee.*

Then he was in a square room. It was day there, or as bright as. People were rushing around. Hospital, he thought. Something was laid over his face, and the light was blocked out. He wasn't sure how long it was out.

Someone leaned over him. "Tristan." The voice broke.

"Dad?"

"Oh, my God, why did you let this happen?"

"Dad, where's Ivy? Is she okay?"

"My God, my God. My child!" his father said.

"Are they helping her?"

His father did not speak.

"Answer me, Dad! Why don't you answer me?"

His father held his face. His father was leaning over him, tears falling down on his face—

My face, Tristan thought with a jolt. That's *my* face.

And yet he was watching his father and himself as if he were standing apart from himself.

"Mr. Carruthers, I'm sorry." A woman in a paramedic's uniform stood next to him and his father.

His father would not look at her. "Dead at the scene?" he asked.

She nodded. "I'm sorry. We didn't have a chance with him."

Tristan felt the darkness coming over him again. He struggled to hold on to consciousness.

"And Ivy?" his father asked.

"Cuts and bruises, in shock. Calling for your son."

Tristan had to find her. He focused on a doorway, concentrated with all his strength, and passed through it. Then another, and another—he was feeling stronger now.

Tristan hurried down the corridor. People kept coming at him. He dodged left and right. He seemed to be going so much faster than they were, and none of them bothered to move out of his way.

A nurse was coming down the hall. He stopped to ask her help in finding Ivy, but she walked past him. He turned a corner and found himself facing a cart loaded with linens. Then he faced the man pushing it. Tristan spun around. The cart and the man were on the other side of him.

Tristan knew that they had passed through him as if he were not there. He had heard what the paramedic said. Still, his mind searched for some other—any other—explanation. But there was none.

He was dead. No one could see him. No one knew he was there. And Ivy would not know.

Tristan felt a pain deeper than any he had ever known. He had told her he loved her, but there had not been time enough to convince her. Now there was no time at all. She'd never believe in his love the way she believed in her angels.

"I said, I can't speak any louder."

Tristan glanced up. He had stopped by a doorway. An old woman was lying in the bed within. She was tiny and gray with long, thin tubes connecting her to machines. She looked like a spider caught in its own web.

"Come in," she said.

He looked behind him to see whom she was talking to.

No one.

"These old eyes of mine are so dim, I can't see my own hand in front of my face," the woman said. "But I can see your light."

Tristan again looked behind him. Her voice sounded certain of what she saw. It seemed much bigger and stronger than her little gray body.

"I knew you would come," she said. "I've been waiting very patiently."

She has been waiting for somebody, Tristan thought, a son or a grandson, and she thinks I'm him. Still, how could she see him if no one else could?

Her face was shining brightly now.

"I've always believed in you," she said. She extended a fragile hand toward Tristan. Forgetting that his hand would pass through hers, he instinctively reached out to her. She closed her eyes.

A moment later, alarms went off. Three nurses rushed into the room. Tristan stepped back as they crowded around the woman. He suddenly realized that they were trying to resuscitate her; he knew they would not. Somehow he knew that the old woman did not want to come back.

Maybe somehow the old woman had known about him.

What did she know?

Tristan could feel the darkness coming over him again. He fought it. What if this time he didn't come back? He had to come back, he had to see Ivy one last time. Desperately he tried to keep himself alert, focusing on one object after another in the room. Then he saw it, next to a small book on the woman's tray: a statue, with a hand outstretched to the woman and angelic wings spread.

For days after, all Ivy could remember was the waterfall of glass. The accident was like a dream she kept having but couldn't remember. Asleep or awake, it would suddenly take over. Her whole body would tense, and her mind would start reeling backward, but all she could remember was the sound of a windshield exploding, then a slow-motion waterfall of glass.

Every day people came and went from the house, Suzanne and Beth, and some other friends and teachers from school. Gary came once; it was a miserable visit for both of them. Will ducked in and out on another day. They brought her flowers, cookies, and sympathy. Ivy couldn't wait until they left, couldn't wait until she could sleep again. But when she lay down at night, she couldn't sleep, and then she had to wait forever until it was day once more.

At the funeral they stood around her, her mother and Andrew on one side, Philip on the other. She let Philip do all the sobbing for her. Gregory stood behind her and from time to time laid his hand on her back. She'd lean against him for a moment. He was the only one who didn't keep asking her to talk about it. He was the only one who seemed to understand her pain and didn't keep telling her that remembering was good for her.

Little by little she did remember—or was told—what had happened. The doctors and police prompted her. The undersides of her arms were full of cuts. She must have held her hands up in front of her face, they said, protecting it from the flying glass. Miraculously, the rest of her injuries were just bruises from the impact and the seat belt restraint. Tristan must have swerved, for the car had swung around to the right, the deer coming in on his side. To protect her, she thought, though the police didn't say that. She told them he had tried to stop but couldn't. It had been twilight. The deer had appeared suddenly. That's all she remembered. Someone told her the car had been totaled, but she refused to look at the newspaper photo.

A week after the funeral, Tristan's mother came to the house and brought a picture of him. She said it was her favorite one. Ivy cradled it in

her hands. He was smiling, wearing his old baseball cap, backward of course, and a ratty school
jacket, looking as Ivy had seen him look so
many times. It seemed as if he were about to ask
her if she wanted to meet for another swimming lesson. For the first time since the accident, Ivy began to cry.

She didn't hear Gregory come into the
kitchen, where she and Tristan's mother were
sitting. When he saw Dr. Carruthers, he demanded to know why she was there.

Ivy showed him Tristan's picture, and he
looked angrily at the woman.

"It's over now," he said. "Ivy is getting over
it. She doesn't need any more reminders."

"When you love someone, it's never over,"
Dr. Carruthers replied gently. "You move on,
because you have to, but you bring him with
you in your heart."

She turned back to Ivy. "You need to talk
and remember, Ivy. You need to cry. Cry hard.
You need to get angry, too. I am!"

"You know," said Gregory, "I'm getting tired
of listening to all this crap. Everyone is telling
Ivy to remember and talk about what happened. Everyone has a pet theory on how to
mourn, but I wonder if they're really thinking
of how it feels for *her.*"

Dr. Carruthers studied him for a moment. "I

wonder if you have really mourned your own loss," she said.

"Don't tell me you're a shrink!"

She shook her head. "Just a person who, like you, has lost someone I loved with all my heart."

Before she left, Tristan's mother asked Ivy if she wanted Ella back.

"I can't have her," Ivy said. "They won't let me!"

Then she ran up to her room, slammed the door, and locked it. One by one, those she loved were being taken away from her.

Picking up an angel statue, one that Beth had just brought her, Ivy hurled it against the wall.

"Why?" she cried out. "Why didn't I die, too?"

She picked up the angel and threw it again.

"You're better off, Tristan. I hate you for being better off than me. You don't miss me now, do you? Oh, no, *you* don't feel a thing!"

On the third try, the angel shattered. Another waterfall of glass. She didn't bother to pick it up.

After dinner that evening, Ivy found the glass cleaned up and the picture of Tristan sitting on her bureau. She didn't ask who had done it. She didn't want to speak to any of them. When Gregory tried to come into her bedroom, she slammed the door in his face. She slammed it in his face again the next morning.

That day, she was barely civil to the customers at 'Tis the Season. When she arrived home, she went straight to her room. Opening the door, she found Philip there, spreading out his baseball cards. She had noticed that he no longer called out the play-by-play for his games, just moved the players silently from base to base. But when he looked up at Ivy, he smiled at her for the first time in days. He pointed to her bed.

"Ella!" Ivy exclaimed. "Ella!"

She hurried in and dropped to her knees beside the bed. Immediately the cat began to purr. Ivy buried her face in the cat's soft fur and started to cry.

Then she felt a light hand on her shoulder. Drying her cheeks on Ella, she turned to Philip. "Does Mom know she's here?"

He nodded. "She knows. It's okay. Gregory said it was. Gregory brought her back to us."

13

When Tristan awakened, he tried to remember which day of the week it was and what lessons he would be giving at the swim camp. Judging by the dim light in his room, it was too early to rise and dress for work. Lying back, he dreamed of Ivy—Ivy with her hair tumbling down.

Slowly he became aware of footsteps outside the door and a sound like something being wheeled by. He leaped up. What was he doing there—lying on the hospital floor in the room of a man he had never seen before? The man yawned and glanced around the room. He did not appear at all surprised by Tristan's presence; he acted as if he didn't even see him.

Then it came back to Tristan: the accident, the ambulance ride, the paramedic's words. He was dead. But he could think. He could watch other people. Was he a ghost?

Tristan remembered the old lady. She had said she saw his light, which was why, he thought, she had mistaken him for an—

"No, no." He said it aloud, but the man didn't hear him. "I can't be that."

Well, whatever he was, he was something that could laugh. He laughed and laughed, almost hysterically. He cried too.

The door behind him swung open suddenly. Tristan quieted himself, but it didn't matter. The nurse who entered was not aware of him, though she stood so close her elbow passed through his as she filled out the man's chart. July 9, 3:45 A.M., Tristan read.

July 9? It couldn't be! It had been June when he'd last been with Ivy. Had he been unconscious for two weeks? Would he black out again? Why was he conscious and there at all?

He thought about the old woman who had reached out to him. Why had she noticed him, but the nurse and others had seen nothing? Would Ivy see him?

Hope surged through Tristan. If he could find Ivy before he fell into the darkness again, he'd have another chance to convince her that he loved her. He would always love her.

The nurse left, shutting the door behind her.

Tristan reached to open it, but his fingers slipped through the handle. He tried again, and again. His hands had no more strength than shadows. Now he'd have to wait for the nurse to come back. He didn't know how long he would stay conscious or whether, like ghosts in old tales, he'd melt away at dawn.

He tried to remember how he had gotten this far and pictured the halls he had traveled down from the emergency room. He could see very clearly the corner where the orderly had gone through him. Suddenly he was traveling the halls to that spot. That was the trick. He had to project a route in his head and focus on where he wanted to go.

Soon he was out on the street. He had forgotten he was at County Hospital and had to get himself all the way home to Stonehill. But he had driven the route a thousand times to pick up his parents. At the thought of them, Tristan slowed down. He remembered his father in the emergency room, leaning over him and weeping. Tristan longed to assure him that everything was all right, but he didn't know how much time would be given to him. His parents had each other; Ivy was alone.

The night sky was just starting to fade into dawn when he arrived at her house. Two rectangles of light glimmered softly in the west wing. Andrew must have been working in his office. Tristan went around back and found the office's French doors thrown open to the cool night air. Andrew was at his desk, deep in thought. Tristan slipped in unseen.

He saw that Andrew's briefcase was open and papers with the college insignia were scattered about. But the document he had been reading was a police report. Tristan realized with a jolt that it was the official report on his and Ivy's accident. Next to it was a newspaper article about them.

The printed words should have made his death more real to him, but they didn't. Instead, they made things that had once counted—his appearance, his swimming record, his school achievements—seem meaningless and small. Only Ivy was important to him now.

She had to know he loved her and that he always would.

He left Andrew to pore over the report, though he didn't understand why he would be so interested in it, and took the back stairs. Slipping past Gregory's room, which was above the office, he crossed the gallery to the hall that led to Ivy's room. He could hardly wait to see her, hardly wait for her to see him. He trembled as he had done before their first swimming lesson. Would they be able to speak to each other?

If anyone could see him and hear him, Ivy could—her faith was strong! Tristan focused on her room and passed through the wall.

Ella sat up immediately. She had been sleeping on Ivy's bed, her thick black fur balled close to Ivy's golden head. Now the cat blinked and stared at him, or at the empty air—after all, cats did that, he thought. But when he moved toward the other side of Ivy's bed, Ella's green eyes followed him.

"Ella, what do you see, Ella?" he asked quietly.

The cat began to purr, and he laughed.

He stood by Ivy's side now. Her hair was tumbled over her face. He tried to brush it back. More than anything he longed to see her face, but his hands were useless.

"I wish you could help me, Ella," he said.

The cat walked over the pillows toward him. He kept very still, wondering what exactly she perceived. Ella leaned as if she would rub against his arm. She fell over sideways and yelped.

Ivy stirred then, and he called her name softly.

Ivy rolled onto her back and he thought she was going to answer him. Her face was a lost moon, beautiful, but pale. All of her light lay in the golden lashes and her long hair spread out like rays from her face.

Ivy frowned. He wanted to smooth the frown away but couldn't. She began to toss and turn.

"Who's there?" she asked. "Who's there?"

He leaned over her. "It's me. Tristan."

"Who's there?" she asked again.

"Tristan!"

Her frown deepened. "I can't see."

He laid his hand on her shoulder, wishing she would awaken, certain that she would see him and hear him. "Ivy, look at me. I'm here!"

Her eyes fluttered open for a moment. Then he saw the change come over her face. He saw the terror take over her. She began to scream.

"Ivy!"

She screamed and screamed.

"Ivy, don't be afraid."

He tried to hold her. He wrapped his arms around her, but their bodies slipped through each other. He could not comfort her.

Then the bedroom door flew open. Philip rushed in. Gregory was close behind him.

"Wake up, Ivy, wake up!" Philip shook her. "Come on, Ivy, please."

Her eyes opened wide now. She gazed at Philip, then glanced around the room. She did not pause at Tristan; she looked straight through him.

Gregory rested his hands lightly on Philip's shoulders and moved him aside. He sat down on the bed, then pulled Ivy close to him. Tristan could see that she was shaking.

"Everything is going to be all right," Gregory said, smoothing back her hair. "It was just a dream."

A terrifying dream, thought Tristan. And he couldn't help her, couldn't comfort her now.

But Gregory could. Tristan was overcome with jealousy.

He couldn't stand to see Gregory holding her that close.

And yet he couldn't stand to see Ivy so frightened and upset. Gratitude to Gregory, as powerful as his jealousy, swept through him. Then jealousy again. Tristan felt weak from this war of feelings and backed away from the three of them, moving toward Ivy's shelves of angels. Ella followed him cautiously.

"Was your dream about the accident?" Philip asked.

Ivy nodded, then dropped her head, running her hands over and over the twisted sheets.

"You want to talk about it?" Gregory asked.

Ivy tried to speak, then shook her head and turned one hand over, palm up. Tristan saw the jagged scars running up her arm like the traces of lightning strikes. For a moment the darkness came up from behind him, but he fought it back.

"I'm here. Everything's okay," Gregory said, and waited patiently.

"I—I was staring at a window," she began. "I saw a large shadow in it, but I wasn't sure who, or what, it was. 'Who's there?' I called out. 'Who's there?'"

From across the room, Tristan watched, her pain and fear pressing upon him.

"I thought it might be someone I knew," she continued. "The shadow looked familiar somehow. So I walked closer, and closer. I couldn't see." She stopped and glanced around the bedroom.

"You couldn't see," prompted Gregory.

"There were other images on the glass, reflections that made it confusing. I got closer. My face was almost against the glass. Suddenly it exploded! The shadow turned into a deer. It crashed through the window and raced away."

She fell silent. Gregory cupped her chin in his hand and pulled it up toward him, gazing deeply into her eyes.

From across the room, Tristan called to her. "Ivy! Ivy, look at me," he begged.

But she looked back at Gregory, her mouth quivering.

"Is that the end of the dream?" Gregory asked.

She nodded.

With the back of his hand he gently stroked her cheek.

Tristan wanted her to be comforted, but—

"You don't remember anything else?" Gregory said.

Ivy shook her head.

"Open your eyes, Ivy! Look at me!" Tristan called to her.

Then he noticed Philip, who was staring at the angel collection—or perhaps at him; he wasn't sure. Tristan put his hand around the statue of the water angel. If only he could find a way to give it to Ivy. If he could send her some sign—

"Come here, Philip," Tristan said. "Come get the statue. Carry it to Ivy."

Philip walked toward the shelves as if drawn by a magnet. Reaching up, he put his hand over Tristan's.

"Look!" Philip cried. "Look!"

"At what?" asked Ivy.

"Your angel. It's glowing."

"Philip, not now," said Gregory.

Philip took the angel down from the shelf and carried it over to her.

"Do you want her by your bed, Ivy?"

"No."

"Maybe she'll keep away bad dreams," he persisted.

"It's just a statue," she said wearily.

"But we can say our prayer, and the real angel will hear it."

"There *are* no real angels, Philip! Don't you understand? If there were, they would have saved Tristan!"

Philip fingered the wings of the statue. He said in a stubborn, little voice, "Angel of light, angel above, take care of me tonight, take care of everyone I love."

"Tell her I'm here, Philip," Tristan said. "Tell her I'm here."

"Look, Ivy!" Philip pointed toward the statues, where Tristan stood. "They're shining!"

"That's enough, Philip!" Gregory said sternly. "Go to bed."

"But—"

"Now!"

When Philip passed by, Tristan held out his hand, but the little boy did not reach back to him. He stared with wonder, not recognition.

What did Philip see? Tristan wondered. Maybe what the old woman had seen: light, some kind of shimmering, but not a shape.

Then he felt the darkness coming on once more. Tristan fought it. He wanted to stay with

Ivy. He could not stand to lose her now. He could not stand to leave her before Gregory did.

What if this was his last time with her? What if he was losing Ivy forever? He struggled desperately to keep back the darkness, but it was rising on all sides now, like a black mist, before him, behind him, closing over his head, and he succumbed.

14

When Tristan awoke from his dreamless dark, the sun was shining brilliantly through Ivy's windows. Her sheets were pulled up and smoothed over with a light comforter. Ivy was gone.

It was the first time Tristan had seen daylight since the accident. He went to the window and marveled at the details of summer, the intricate designs of leaves, the way the wind could run a finger through the grass and send a green wave over the top of the ridge. The wind. Though the curtains were moving, Tristan couldn't feel its cool touch. Though the room was streaked with sun, he couldn't feel its warmth.

Ella could. The cat was lying on a T-shirt of

Ivy's tucked in a bright corner. She greeted Tristan by opening one eye and purring a little.

"Not much dirty laundry lying around here for you, is there?" he asked, thinking of the cat's fondness for his smelliest socks and sweats. The stillness of the house made him speak quietly, though he knew he could shout loud enough to—well, loud enough to wake the dead, and only he would hear.

The loneliness was intense. Tristan feared that he would always be alone this way, wandering and never seen, never heard, never known as Tristan. Why hadn't he seen the old lady from the hospital after she died? Where had she gone?

Dead people went to cemeteries, he thought as he crossed the hallway to the stairs. Then he stopped in his tracks. He had a grave somewhere! Probably next to his grandparents. He hurried down the steps, curious to see what they had done with him. Perhaps he'd also find the old woman or someone else recently dead who could make sense of all this.

Tristan had visited Riverstone Rise Cemetery several times when he was a little boy. It had never seemed a sad place to him, perhaps because the sites of his grandparents' graves had always inspired his father to tell Tristan interesting and funny stories about them. His mother had spent the time trimming and planting. Tristan had run and climbed stones and broad-jumped the graves, using the cemetery as a kind of playground and obstacle course. But that seemed centuries ago.

It was strange now to slip through the tall iron gates—gates he had swung on like a little monkey, his mother always said—in search of his own grave. Whether he moved from memory or instinct, he wasn't sure, but he found his way quickly to the lower path and around the bend marked by three pines. He knew it was fifteen feet farther and prepared himself for the shock of reading his own name on the stone next to his grandparents'.

But he didn't even glance at it. He was too astonished by the presence of a girl who had stretched out and made herself quite at home on the freshly upturned dirt.

"Excuse me," he said, knowing full well that people didn't hear him. "You're lying on my grave."

She glanced upward then, which made him wonder if he was shimmering again. The girl was about his age and looked vaguely familiar to him.

"You must be Tristan," she said. "I knew you'd show up sooner or later."

Tristan stared at her.

"You're him, right?" she said, sitting up, indicating his name with a jab of her thumb. "Recently dead, right?"

"Recently alive," he said. There was something about her attitude that made him want to argue with her.

She shrugged. "Everybody has his own point of view."

He couldn't get over the fact that she could hear him. "And you," he said, studying her rather unusual looks, "what are you?"

"Not so recently."

"I see. Is that why your hair is that color?"

Her hand flew up to her head. "Ex*cuse* me?"

The hair was short, dark, and spiky, and had a strange magenta tinge, a purplish hue, as if the henna rinse had gone wrong.

"That's what color it was when I died."

"Oh. Sorry."

"Have a seat," she said, patting the newly mounded earth. "After all, it's your resting place. I was just crashing for a while."

"So you're a . . . a ghost," he said.

"Ex*cuse* me?"

He wished she'd stop using that annoying tone.

"Did you say 'ghost'? You *are* recent. We're not ghosts, sweetie." She tapped his arm several times with a long, pointed, purplish black nail.

Again he wondered if this was from being "not recently" dead but was afraid she'd puncture him if he asked.

Then he realized that her hand did not pass through his. They were indeed made of the same stuff.

"We're angels, sweetie. *That's right.* Heaven's little helpers."

Her tone and tendency to exaggerate certain words were starting to grate on his nerves.

She pointed toward the sky. "Someone's got a wicked sense of humor. Always chooses the least likely."

"I don't believe it," Tristan said. "I don't believe it."

"So this is the first time you've seen your new digs. Missed your own funeral, huh? *That,*" she said, "was a very big mistake. I enjoyed *every minute* of mine."

"Where are you buried?" Tristan asked, looking around. The stone on one side of his family plot had a carving of a lamb, which hardly seemed right for her, and on the other side, a serene-looking woman with hands folded over her breasts and eyes lifted toward heaven—an equally bad choice.

"I'm not buried. That's why I'm subletting from you."

"I don't understand," said Tristan.

"Don't you recognize me?"

"Uh, no," he said, afraid she was going to tell him she was related to him somehow, or maybe that he had chased her in sixth grade.

"Look at me from this side." She showed him her profile.

Tristan looked at her blankly.

"Boy, you didn't have much of a life, did you, when you had a life," she remarked.

"What do you mean?"

"You didn't go out much."

"All the time," Tristan replied.

"Didn't go to the movies."

"I went all the time," Tristan argued.

"But you never saw any of Lacey Lovitt's films."

"Sure I did. Everybody did, before she— You're Lacey Lovitt?"

She rolled her eyes upward. "I hope you're faster at figuring out your mission."

"I guess it's just that your hair color is different."

"We've already talked about my hair," she said, scrambling up from the grave. It was odd to see her standing against the background of trees. The willows waved ropes of leaves in the breeze, but her hair lay as still as a girl's in a photograph.

"I remember now," Tristan said. "Your plane

went down over the ocean. They never found you."

"Imagine how pleased I was to find myself climbing out of New York Harbor."

"The accident was two years ago, wasn't it?"

At that, she ducked her head. "Yeah, well . . ."

"I remember reading about your funeral," Tristan said. "Lots of famous people went."

"And lots of almost-famous. People are always looking for publicity." There was a bitter edge to her voice. "I wish you could have seen my mother, weeping and wailing." Lacey struck a pose like the marble figure of a woman weeping in the next row over. "You would have thought she had lost someone she loved."

"Well, she did if you're her daughter."

"You *are* naive, aren't you." It was a statement rather than a question. "You could have learned something about people if you had gone to your own funeral. Maybe you still can learn. There's a burial on the east side this morning. Let's go," she said.

"Go to a burial? Isn't that kind of morbid?"

She laughed at him over her shoulder. "Nothing can be morbid, Tristan, once you're dead. Besides, I find them highly entertaining. And when they're not, I make them so, and you look like you could use some cheering up. Come on."

"I think I'll pass."

She turned and studied him for a minute, perplexed. "All right. How about this: I saw a group of girls come in earlier, headed for the ritzy side of town. Maybe you'd enjoy that more. Good audiences, you know, are hard to come by, especially when you're dead and most of them can't see you."

She began pacing around in a circle.

"Yeah, that'll be much better." She seemed to be talking to herself as much as him. "It will score me some points." She glanced over at Tristan. "You see, fooling around with funeral parties doesn't really meet with approval. But with this, I'll be performing a service. Next time those girls will think twice about respect for the dead."

Tristan had hoped that another person like him would clear things up a bit, but—

"Oh, cheer up, Dumps!" She started down the road.

Tristan followed slowly and tried to remember if he had ever read that Lacey Lovitt was crazy.

She led him to an older section of the cemetery where there were family plots owned by longtime, wealthier residents of Stonehill. On one side of the road, mausoleums with facades like miniature temples sank their backs into the hill. On the other side were gardenlike squares with tall, polished monuments and a variety of marble statues. Tristan had been there before. At Maggie's request, Caroline had been buried in the Baines family plot.

"Swanky, huh?"

"I'm surprised you sublet from me," Tristan remarked.

"Oh, I made millions in my time," said Lacey. "Millions. But at heart I'm a simple girl from New York's Lower East Side. I started with the soaps, remember, and then—but no need to go into all that. I'm sure, now that you recognize me, you know all about me."

Tristan didn't bother to correct her.

"So, what do you think those girls had in mind?" she asked, stopping to look around. There was no one in sight, just smooth stones, bright flowers, and a sea of lush grass.

"I was wondering the same thing about you," he replied.

"Oh, I'll just improvise. I doubt you'll be much help. You couldn't have any real skills yet. Probably all you can do is stand there and shimmer, like some kind of freakin' Christmas ornament—meaning only a believer or two will see you."

"Only a believer?"

"You mean you still haven't figured out *that?*" She shook her head in disbelief.

But he had figured it out; he just didn't want to admit it, just didn't want it to be true. The old lady had been a believer. So was Philip. Both of them had seen him shimmering. But Ivy had not. Ivy had stopped believing.

"You can do something more than shimmer?" Tristan asked hopefully.

She looked at him as if he were utterly stupid. "What on earth do you think I've been doing for the last two years?"

"I have no idea," Tristan said.

"*Don't* tell me, *puh-lease* don't tell me I'm going to have to explain to you about missions."

He ignored the melodramatics. "You mentioned that before. What missions?"

"Your mission, my mission," she replied quickly. "We each have a mission. And we have to fulfill it if we want to get on to where everyone else has gone." She started walking again, rather quickly, and he had to hurry to catch up.

"But what is my mission?"

"How should I know?"

"Well, somebody has to tell me. How can I fulfill it if I have no idea what it is?" he said, frustrated.

"Don't complain to me about it!" she snapped. "It's your job to find out." In a quieter voice she added, "It's usually some kind of unfinished business. Sometimes it's someone you know who needs your help."

"So I have at least two years to—"

"Well, no, that's not exactly how it works," she said, making that funny ducking motion with her head that he had seen before. She moved ahead of him, then passed through a black iron fence whose curled and rusted spikes made odd designs against the walls of an old stone chapel. "Let's find the kids."

"Wait a minute," he said, reaching for her arm. She was the one thing that he could grab hold of. "You've got to tell me. How *exactly* does this mission thing work?"

"Well . . . well, you're supposed to find out and complete your mission as soon as possible. Some angels take a few days, some angels take a few months."

"And you've been at it for two years," he said. "How close are you to completing yours?"

She ran her tongue over her teeth. "Don't know."

"Great," he said. "Great! I don't know what I'm doing, and I've finally found myself a guide, only she's taking eight times as long as everybody else."

"Twice as long!" she said. "Once I met an angel who took a year. You see, Tristan, I get a little distracted. I'm going about my business, and I see these opportunities that are just too good to pass by. Some of them don't really meet with approval."

"Some of them? Like what?" Tristan asked suspiciously.

She shrugged. "Once I dropped a stage chandelier on my jerky ex-director's head—just missing, of course. He always was a big fan of *Phantom of the Opera*—that's what I mean by an opportunity just too good to pass by. And that's how it usually goes for me. I'm two points closer, then something comes up, and I'm three points back and never quite getting to figuring out my mission.

"But don't worry—you probably have more discipline than me. For you, it'll be a snap."

I'm going to wake up, Tristan thought, and this nightmare will be over. Ivy will be lying in my arms—

"How much do you want to bet that those girls are in the chapel?"

Tristan eyed the gray stone building. Its doors had been bound with heavy chains since he was a little boy.

"Is there a way in?"

"For us, there is always a way in. For them, a broken window in the back. Any special requests?"

"What?"

"Anything you'd like to see me do?"

Wake me up, thought Tristan. "Uh, no."

"You know, I don't know what's on your mind, Trist, but you're acting deader than dead."

Then she slipped through the wall. Tristan followed.

The chapel was dark except for one square of luminescent green where the window was broken in the back. Dry leaves and crumbling plaster were scattered over its floor, along with broken bottles and cigarettes. Wooden benches were carved over with initials and blackened with symbols that Tristan couldn't decipher.

The girls, whom he judged to be about eleven or twelve, were seated in a circle in the altar area and giggling with nervousness.

"Okay, who are we going to call back?" one of them asked. They glanced at one another, then over their shoulders.

"Jackie Onassis," said a girl with a brown ponytail.

"Kurt Cobain," another suggested.

"My grandmother."

"My great-uncle Lennie."

"I know!" said a tiny, freckle-faced blonde. "How about Tristan Carruthers?"

Tristan blinked.

"Too bloody," said the leader.

"Yeah," said the brunette, pulling her pony-tail up into two long pieces. "He'd probably have antlers coming out of the back of his head."

"Ew, gross!"

Lacey snickered.

"My sister had the biggest crush on him," the freckled blonde said.

Lacey batted her eyelashes at Tristan.

"One time, like, when we were fooling around at the pool, he, like, blew the whistle at us. It was cool."

"He was a hunk!"

Lacey stuck her finger down her throat and rolled her eyes.

"Still, he might be bloody," said a redhead. "Who else can we call for?"

"Lacey Lovitt."

The girls looked around at each other. Which one of them had said it?

"I remember her. She was in *Dark Moon Running*."

"*Dark Moon Rising*."

It was Lacey's voice, Tristan realized, sounding the same but different, the way a televised voice was the same but different than a live one. Somehow she was producing it in a way that they all could hear.

The girls looked around, a little spooked.

"Let's join hands," the leader said. "We're calling back Lacey Lovitt. If you're here, Lacey, give us a sign."

"I never liked Lacey Lovitt."

Tristan saw Lacey's eyes spark.

"Shhh. The spirits are around us now."

"I see them!" said the little blonde. "I see their light! Two of them."

"So do I!"

"I don't," said the girl with the brown ponytail.

"Let's get somebody other than Lacey Lovitt."

"Yeah, she was obnoxious."

It was Tristan's turn to snicker.

"I like that new girl in *Dark Moon*. The one who took her place."

"Me too," the redhead agreed.

"She's a much better actress. And she has better hair."

Tristan's laughter softened. He glanced warily at Lacey.

"Well, she's not dead," said the leader. "We're calling Lacey Lovitt. If you're here, Lacey, give us a sign."

It began with a slow whirling of dust. Tristan saw that Lacey herself became faint as the dust whirled upward. Then the dust drifted off and she was there again, running around the outside of the circle, pulling hair.

The girls shrieked and held their heads. She pinched two of them, then picked up their sweaters and hurled them this way and that.

By this time the girls were on their feet, still screaming, and running for the open window.

Empty bottles flew over their heads and smashed against the chapel wall.

In a moment the girls were gone, their screams trailing behind them like thin, birdlike calls.

"Well," said Tristan when it was quiet again, "I guess everyone should be glad that there wasn't a chandelier in here. Feeling better?"

"Little snips!"

"How did you do that?" he asked.

"I've seen that new actress. She stinks."

"I'm sure," said Tristan, "that she can't be nearly as dramatic as you. You were pulling and throwing. How did you do that? I can't use my hands at all."

"Figure it out for yourself!" She was still fuming. "Better hair!" She pulled on strands of the purplish stuff. "This is my own personal style." She glared at Tristan.

He smiled back.

"As for how I use my hands," she said, "do you really think I'd take up *my* precious time to teach *you?*"

Tristan nodded. "Good audiences are hard

to come by," he reminded her, "especially when you're dead and most of them can't see you."

Then he left her sulking in the chapel. He figured she'd know how to locate him and would when she was ready.

Out in the noonday sun again, Tristan blinked. While he did not feel changes in temperature, he did seem very sensitive to light and darkness. In the darkened chapel he had seen auras around the girls, and now, in the tree-shaded landscape, splotches of sunlight seemed dazzlingly bright.

Perhaps that was why he mistook the visitor for Gregory. The way he moved, the dark hair, and the shape of his head convinced Tristan that Gregory was walking away from the Baines family plot. Then the visitor, as if he sensed someone watching him, turned around.

He was much older than Gregory, forty or so, and his face was twisted with grief. Tristan reached out a hand to him, but the man turned away and continued on.

So did Tristan, but not before he noticed, on the fresh green belly of Caroline's grave, a long-stemmed red rose.

15

Lacey found Tristan again late that afternoon. She called his name, startling him as he walked along the edge of the ridge. He looked up to see her sitting in a tree.

"Nice view, isn't it?" said Lacey.

Tristan nodded, and gazed again down the stony drop. The land fell away steeply there for two or three hundred feet. He remembered seeing in the early spring the silver tracks and the roof of the one-room train station in the valley below, but now they were hidden. Only small flecks of river could be seen flashing blue through the trees. "I don't know why I'm so drawn to this place."

Lacey cocked her head. "I'm sure that it has *nothing* to do with the fact that Ivy lives here," she said sarcastically.

"How did you know about Ivy?"

The girl did a neat skin-the-cat and dropped down from the tree.

"Read about her, of course." Lacey walked along next to him. "Read all about your accident. I make it a habit to drop by the station every morning and read the paper with the commuters. Don't like to be out of the skinny. Besides, it helps me to keep the date straight."

"Today's Sunday, July tenth," Tristan said.

"Brrrrrrt!" She made a sound like a game-show buzzer, and snapped a twig from the tree. "Tuesday, July twelfth."

"Couldn't be," Tristan said. He reached up but couldn't pull off a leaf, much less snap a branch.

"Did you fall into the darkness in the last couple of days?"

"Last night," he replied.

"More like three nights ago," she told him. "That will happen, but eventually you'll build up your strength and need less and less rest. Except, of course, when you do fancy jobs."

"Fancy jobs. Like what?"

She waited till she had his full attention, then said, "Look at me."

"What do you think I'm doing?"

"Stand back a little and look harder. What am I missing?"

"Do you promise not to pull my hair?"

She scowled at him. It was a fine scowl, but it passed quickly—she was just acting.

"Look at that cat," she said.

He glanced over his shoulder. "Ella!"

"Look at the grass next to the cat and look at the grass next to me."

He saw it then. "You have no shadow."

"Neither do you."

"You're talking out loud," he observed. "I recognize that sound and saw Ella's ears flick in your direction."

"Now watch the grass behind me," she instructed, and closed her eyes. Slowly, like dark water seeping over the lawn, her shadow grew. Just as slowly she lost her shimmering quality. Ella cautiously circled her once, twice. Then she rubbed against Lacey's leg and didn't fall over.

"You're solid!" Tristan exclaimed. "Solid! Anybody could see you! Teach me how to do it. If I can make myself solid, Ivy will see me, she'll know I'm here for her, she'll know—"

"Whoa," Lacey cut in. Then her projected voice began to fade. "I'll be with you in a minute."

Her shadow disappeared. Then she did—completely.

"Lacey?" Tristan spun around. "Lacey, where are you? Are you all right?"

"Just tired." Her voice was small. Her body appeared again but was almost translucent. She lay curled in a ball on the ground. "Give me a few minutes."

Tristan paced back and forth, eyeing her worriedly.

Suddenly she sprang up, looking like herself again. "It's like this," she said. "For transient angels—that's you and me, sweetie—it takes all the energy we have and a lot of experience to materialize completely. To speak at the same time— well, only a professional can do that."

"Meaning you," he said.

"Usually I just materialize part of myself, such as my fingers, when I want to do something—pull hair or turn the paper to the movie reviews."

"Teach me!" Tristan said fervently. "Will you show me how?"

"Maybe."

They had come around to a full view of the back of the house. Tristan gazed up at the dormer window that looked out from Ivy's music room.

"So this is where the chick lives," Lacey said. "I suppose I should think it refreshing that a guy would let himself be such a fool over a girl."

He saw Lacey's lips curl back in distaste.

"I don't see why you should think anything. It's got nothing to do with you," Tristan replied. "Are you going to teach me?"

"Oh, why not? I have time to kill."

They searched out a hidden nook in the trees and sat down, Ella following slowly behind them. Lacey began to pet the cat, and Ella rewarded her with a small, polite purr. When Tristan looked closely, he could see that the tips of her fingers did not glow. They were quite solid.

"All it requires is concentration," said Lacey. "Intense concentration. Look at your fingertips, stare at them as a way of maintaining your focus. You almost will them into being."

Tristan extended his hand toward Ella. He forced everything else out of his mind, focusing on his fingertips. He felt a slight tingling sensation, the kind of pins-and-needles feeling he used to get when his arm fell asleep. The sensation grew stronger and stronger in his fingers. Then another kind of tingling began in his head, a feeling he did not like. He started to grow faint. His whole self, except for his fingers, felt like it was melting away. He pulled back.

Lacey clucked at him. "Lost your nerve."

"I'll try again."

"Better rest for a sec."

"I don't need rest!"

It was humiliating, after being strong and smart all his life—the swimming teacher, the math tutor—to accept lessons from this know-it-all girl on something as simple as petting a cat.

"Looks like I'm not the only one around here with a big ego," Lacey observed with satisfaction.

Tristan ignored the comment. "What was happening to me?" he asked.

"All your energy was being rerouted to your fingertips," she said, "which made the rest of you feel faint, or like you were dissolving or something."

He nodded.

"As you build up your strength that won't be a problem," she added. "If you ever get to the point of materializing your whole self and projecting your voice—though, frankly, I doubt you will—you'll have to learn to draw energy from your surroundings. I just suck it right out of there."

"You sound like an alien in a sci-fi horror movie."

She nodded. "*Lips of Planet Indigo.* You know, I came this close to winning an Oscar for that."

Funny, Tristan remembered it as a box-office bomb.

"Want to try again now?"

Tristan extended his hand. In a way, it was like finding his pulse, like lying on a bed and hearing his own heart: he suddenly became aware of the way energy traveled through him, and he directed it, this time coolly and calmly, to his fingertips. They lost their shimmer.

Then he felt her. Soft, silky, deep fur. Ella began to purr loudly as he traced out all her favorite places to be petted. She rolled on her back. Tristan laughed. When he scratched her belly, her "motor" seemed as loud as a small prop plane's.

Then he lost the touch. The sunlit day went gray. Ella stopped purring. All he could do was hold still and wait, sucking on the air around him like someone trying to catch his breath, though he had none.

"Excellent!" said Lacey. "I had no idea I was such a good teacher."

Color returned to the grass and trees. The sky burned blue again. Only Ella, scrambling to her feet and sniffing the air, showed signs that something wasn't quite right.

Tristan turned to Lacey, exhausted. "I won't be able to reach her. If that is as much as I can do, I won't be able to reach her."

"Are we talking about the chick again?"

"You know her name."

"Ivy. Symbol of faithfulness and remembering. Is there some message you're trying to send her?"

"I have to convince her that I love her."

"That's it?" Lacey made a face. "*That's it?*"

"I think it's probably my mission," Tristan said.

"Oh, *puh-lease.*"

"You know, I'm getting pretty tired of your sarcasm," Tristan told her.

"I don't much enjoy your silliness," she replied. "Tristan, you are naive if you think the Number One Director would go to all the trouble of making you an angel so you could convince some chick that you love her. Missions are never that simple, never that easy."

He wanted to fight with her, but her melodramatic hand-waving had ceased. She was serious.

"I still don't get it," he said. "How am I supposed to discover my mission?"

"You watch. You listen. You stay close to the people you know or the people you feel yourself drawn to—they're probably the people you've been sent back to help."

Tristan began to wonder who in his life might need special help.

"It's sort of like being a detective," Lacey said. "The hitch is, it's not just a whodunit. It's a who-done-*what*. Often you don't know what the problem is that you've been sent to solve. Sometimes the problem hasn't happened yet—you have to save the person from some disaster that is going to occur in the future."

"You're right," said Tristan. "It's not simple."

They had walked their way past the tennis court and around to the front of the house. Ella, who had been following them, scurried ahead and up the front steps.

"Even if it is something that will happen in the future," Lacey went on, "the key is often hidden in your own past. Fortunately, time travel is not that hard."

Tristan raised his eyebrows. "Time travel?"

Lacey hopped up on Gregory's car, which had been left in the driveway in front of the house.

"Traveling backward in your mind, I mean. There are a lot of things we forget if we remember only in the present. There may be clues that we didn't pick up in the past, but they're still there and can be found again by traveling backward in our minds."

As Lacey spoke she stretched out on the hood of the BMW. She looked to Tristan like Morticia Addams doing a car ad.

"Maybe," she baited him, "I'll teach you how to travel through time, too. Of course, traveling backward in someone *else's* mind, that's not something for an amateur like you to fool around with. There is some danger in all of this," she added. "Oh, cheer *up,* Dumps."

"I'm not down. I'm thinking."

"Then *look* up," she said.

Tristan glanced toward the front door. Ivy stood there, looking out toward the driveway, as if waiting for someone.

"'It is my lady, O, it is my love! O, that she knew she were!'" said Lacey.

Tristan kept his eyes on Ivy. "What?"

"*Romeo and Juliet.* Act two, scene two. I auditioned for it, you know, for Shakespeare in the Park. The casting director wanted me."

"Good," Tristan said vaguely. He wished she'd leave him alone now. All he wanted was to be alone, to revel in the sight of Ivy, Ivy stepping out onto the porch, Ivy with her hair blowing gold as she gracefully moved to the top of the steps and picked up Ella.

"The director said my kind of talent was to die for."

"Great," said Tristan. If only cats could talk, he thought. Tell her, Ella, tell her what you know.

"The producer, a *major artsy-fartsy,* said he wanted someone who had a 'more classic' face, someone with a voice that wouldn't lapse into New Yorkese."

Ivy was still standing on the porch, cuddling Ella and looking toward him. Maybe she did believe, Tristan thought. Maybe she had a faint sense of his presence.

"That producer is in New York for a couple of weeks, getting a road show ready. I thought I'd pay him a visit."

"Great," Tristan repeated. He turned his head when Ivy did, hearing the whine of a small car climbing to the top of the hill.

"I thought I'd murder him," Lacey added, "cause a traffic accident that would kill him on the spot."

"Terrific."

"You're pathetic!" she said. "You're really pathetic! Were you this gaga in life? I can only imagine you when you still had hormones pumping through you."

He turned to her angrily. "Look," he said, "you're no better than I am. I'm in love with Ivy, you're in love with you. We're both obsessed, so back off."

For a moment Lacey didn't say anything. Her eyes changed ever so slightly. A camera would not have caught the flicker of hurt feelings. But Tristan did, and knowing that this time she wasn't acting, he regretted his words.

"I'm sorry."

Lacey had turned away from him. He figured she'd be off anytime now, leaving him to fumble his way through his mission.

"Lacey, I'm sorry."

"Well, well, well," she said.

"It's just that—"

"Who is this?" she interrupted him. "Tweedledee and Tweedledum come to mourn with your lady?"

He turned to watch Beth and Suzanne get out of the car. As it happened, they were both wearing black, but Suzanne had always liked black, especially scanty black, which was what she was wearing—a cool halter-top dress. Beth, on the other hand, was wearing clothes typical of Beth: a loose shift, black with small white flowers on it, whose ruffled hem blew a couple of inches above her red plastic sandals.

"They're her friends, Beth and Suzanne."

"That one is definitely a radio," said Lacey.

"A radio?"

"The one who looks like she's wearing a shower curtain."

"Beth," he said. "She's a writer."

"What'd I tell you? A born radio."

Tristan watched Ivy greet her friends and lead them into the house.

"Let's go," Lacey said, springing forward. "This is going to be fun."

He hung back. He had seen her kind of fun earlier.

"Do you want to tell her you love her, or don't you? This will be good training for you, Tristan. You've got it made, the girl's an absolute radio. Good radios don't even have to believe," she added. "They are receptive to all kinds of things, one of those things being angels. You can speak through her—at least, you can write through her. You know what automatic writing is, don't you?"

He had heard of it. Mediums did it, their hands supposedly writing at the will of someone else, relaying messages from the dead.

"You mean Beth is like a medium?"

"An untrained one. A natural radio. She'll broadcast you—if not today, then tomorrow. We've just got to establish the link and slip into her mind."

"Slip into her mind?" he asked.

"It's pretty simple," Lacey said. "All you need to do is think exactly like her, see the world the way Beth sees it, feel as Beth feels, love whomever she loves, desire her deepest desires."

"No way," said Tristan.

"In short, you have to adopt the radio's point of view, and then you slip right in."

"You obviously don't know the way Beth's mind works," said Tristan. "You've never seen her stories. She writes these torrid romances."

"Oh. . . you mean the kind where the lover stares longingly at his beloved, his eyes soulful, his heart aching so that he cannot see or hear anyone else?"

"Exactly."

She tilted back her head and smirked. "You're right. You and Beth are certainly different."

Tristan didn't say anything.

"If you really loved Ivy, you'd try. I'm sure the lovers in Beth's stories wouldn't let a little challenge like this stop them."

"How about Philip?" said Tristan. "He's Ivy's brother. And he can see me shimmering."

"Ah! You've found a believer," she said.

"A radio, I'm sure," Tristan told her.

"Not necessarily. There's no real connection between believing and being a radio."

"Can't we try him first?"

"Sure, we can waste time," she said, and slipped inside the house.

Philip was in the kitchen making microwave brownies. On the counter next to his bowl were a few sticky baseball cards and a catalogue opened to a picture of kids' mountain bikes. Tristan was confident. This was a point of view he knew well.

"Stay behind him," Lacey advised. "If he notices your glow, it will distract him. He'll start searching and trying to understand. He'll focus outward so hard that he won't be open to letting anything else in."

Actually, staying behind Philip helped in other ways. Tristan read the box directions over Philip's shoulder. He thought about what step he should do next and how the brownies would smell as they baked, how they would taste, warm and crumbly, just out of the oven. He wanted to lick the spoon, with its raw, runny chocolate. Philip did lick it.

Tristan knew who he was, and at the same time he was someone else too, the way he'd felt sometimes when reading a good story. This was easy. "Philip, it's me—"

Wham! Tristan reeled backward, as if he had walked into a glass wall. He hadn't seen it, had been totally unaware of it, till it slammed him in the face. For a few moments, he was stunned.

"It can get pretty rough sometimes," Lacey said, observing him. "I guess it's clear to you now. Philip doesn't want you in."

"But I was his friend."

"He doesn't know it's you."

"If he'd let me talk to him, then he would know," Tristan argued.

"It doesn't work that way," she said. "I warned you. I'm getting good at telling radios from non-radios. You can try him again, but he'll be ready for you this time, and it will be even tougher. You don't want a radio who fights you. Let's try Beth."

Tristan paced around. "Why don't *you* try Beth?"

"Sorry."

"But"—he thought fast—"you're such a great actress, Lacey. That's why this kind of thing comes easily to you. An actress's job is to take on a role. The really great ones, *like you,* don't just imitate. No, they *become* the other person. That's why you do it so well."

"Nice try," she said. "But Beth is your radio to the one you're messaging. You have to do it yourself. That's just the way it works."

"It never seems to work the way I want it to," he complained.

"You've noticed that too," she remarked. "I assume you know how to get up to your lady's bower."

Tristan led the way to Ivy's bedroom. The door was open a crack. Ella, who was still following them, nudged it open and entered; they passed through the walls.

Suzanne was sitting in front of Ivy's mirror, rifling through an open jewelry box, trying on Ivy's necklaces and earrings. Ivy was sprawled out on her bed, reading a sheaf of papers—one of Beth's stories, Tristan figured. Beth was pacing around the room.

"At least get yourself a jewel-encrusted pencil," Suzanne said, "if you're going to continue to wear it in your hair like that."

Beth reached up to the knot of hair wound high on her head and plucked out a pencil. "I forgot."

"You're getting worse and worse, Beth."

"It's just all so interesting. Courtney swears her little sister is telling the truth. And when some of the guys went back to the chapel, they found one of the girls' sweaters hung high up on a sconce."

"The girls themselves could have thrown it up there," Suzanne pointed out.

"Mmm. Maybe," Beth said, and pulled a notebook out of her purse.

Lacey turned to Tristan. "There's your entrance. She's thinking about this morning. Couldn't have been laid out easier for you."

Beth rolled her pencil back and forth between her fingers. Tristan moved close to her. Guessing that she was trying to picture the scene, he recalled the way the chapel had looked, moving from the bright light outside into its tall shadowiness. He saw the girls settling themselves in the altar area. Beth's stories always had a million details. He recalled the crumbling debris on the floor and imagined how the damp stone might feel beneath the girls' bare legs, how their skin might prickle if a draft came through the broken window, or how they'd twitch if they thought they felt a spider on their legs.

He was in the scene, slipping out of himself and into— Whoa! She didn't slam down like Philip, but he was pushed back swiftly and firmly. Beth stood up, moved several feet away, and looked back at the spot where she had been writing.

"Does she see me?" Tristan asked Lacey. "Does she see my glow?"

"I don't think so—she's not paying any attention to mine. But she knows something's going on. You came on too strong."

"I was trying to think the way she would think, giving her some details. She loves details."

"You rushed her. She knows it doesn't feel right. Back off a little."

But Beth started writing then, describing the girls in the circle. Some of his details were there—whether by his suggestion or her own creation, he wasn't sure—but he couldn't resist pushing further.

Slam! This time it came down hard, so hard that Tristan actually fell backward.

"I warned you," said Lacey.

"Beth, you are as nervous as a cat," Suzanne said.

Ivy looked up from her story. "As nervous as Ella? She's been acting really funny lately."

Lacey shook her finger at Tristan. "Listen to me. You've got to go easy. Imagine Beth is a house and you're a thief breaking in. You have to take your time. You have to creep. Find what you need in the basement, in her unconscious, but don't disturb the person living upstairs. Got it?"

He got it, but he was reluctant to try again. The strength of Beth's mind and the directness of her blow was much greater than Philip's.

Tristan felt frustrated, unable to send the simplest message to Ivy. She was so close, so close, yet . . . He could pass his hand through hers, but never touch. Lie next to her, but never comfort. Say a line to make her smile, but never be heard. He had no place in her life now, and perhaps that was better for her, but it was life in death for him.

"Wow!" said Beth. "Wow—if I do say so myself! How's this for the first line of a story: 'He had no place in her life now, and perhaps that was better for her, but it was life in death for him.'"

Tristan saw the words on the page as if he were holding the notebook in his own hands. And when Beth turned to gaze at the picture of him on Ivy's bureau, he turned, too.

If only you knew, he thought

"'If only,'" she wrote. "If only, if only, if only . . ." She seemed to be stuck.

"That is a good beginning," Ivy said, setting aside the typed story. "What comes after it?"

"'If only.'"

"If only what?" Suzanne asked.

"I don't know," Beth said.

Tristan saw the room through her eyes, how pretty it was, how Ella was staring at her, how Suzanne and Ivy exchanged glances, then shrugged.

If only Ivy knew how I love her. He thought the words as clearly as possible.

"'If only I freed—'" She stopped writing and frowned. He could feel the puzzlement like a crease in his own mind.

"Ivy, Ivy, Ivy," he said. "If only Ivy."

"Beth, you look so pale," Ivy observed. "Are you okay?"

Beth blinked several times. "It's as if someone else is making up words for me."

Suzanne made little whistling sounds.

"I am not cuckoo!" said Beth.

Ivy walked over to Beth and looked into her

eyes; she gazed straight in at him. But he knew she didn't see.

"'But she didn't see,'" Beth wrote. Then she scratched out and rewrote, reading aloud as she went: "'He had no place in her life, and perhaps that was best for her, but it was a miserable life in death for him. If only she'd free . . . him from his prison of love. But she didn't know, didn't see the key that was in her hands only—' Beth lifted her pencil for a moment. "I'm on a roll now!" she exclaimed.

She started writing again. "'In her gentle, loving, caring, caressing, hands, in hands that held, that healed, that hoped—'"

Oh, come on, thought Tristan.

"Shut up," Beth answered him.

"What?" said Ivy, her eyes opening wide.

"You're glowing."

Everyone turned to look at Philip, who was standing outside Ivy's door.

"You're glowing, Beth," Philip said.

Ivy turned away. "Philip, I told you I don't want to hear any more about that."

"About me glowing?" Beth asked.

"He's into this angel stuff," Ivy explained. "He claims he sees colors and things, and thinks they're angels. I can't stand it anymore! I don't want to hear it anymore! How many times do I have to tell you that?"

Hearing her words, Tristan lost heart. His effort had taken him well past exhaustion; hope was all that had been sustaining him. Now that was gone.

Beth jerked her head, and he was outside of her once more. Philip kept his eyes on Tristan, following him as he joined Lacey.

"Gee," said Suzanne, winking at Beth, "I wonder where Philip learned about angels."

"They've helped you in the past, Ivy," Beth said gently. "Why can't they help him now?"

"They didn't help me!" Ivy exclaimed. "If angels were real, if angels were our guardians, Tristan would be alive! But he's gone. How can I still believe in angels?"

Her hands were curled into two tight fists. The stormy look in her eyes had become an intense green, burning with certainty, the certainty that there were no angels.

Tristan felt as if he were dying all over again.

Suzanne looked at Beth and shrugged. Philip said nothing. Tristan saw that familiar set in his jaw.

"He's a stubborn little bugger," Lacey remarked.

Tristan nodded. Philip was still believing. Tristan let himself hope just a little.

Then Ivy pulled a plastic bag out of her

trash can. She started clearing off her shelves of angels.

"Ivy, no!"

But his words wouldn't stop her.

Philip tugged on her arm. "Can I have them?" She ignored him.

"Can I have them, Ivy?"

Tristan heard the glass breaking inside the bag. Her hand moved steadily, relentlessly down the line, but she hadn't touched Tony or the water angel yet.

"Please, Ivy."

At last she stopped. "All right. You can have them," she said, "but you have to promise me, Philip, that you will never speak to me about angels again."

Philip looked up thoughtfully at the last two angels. "Okay. But what if—"

"No," she said firmly. "That's the deal.'

He carefully took down Tony and the water angel. "I promise."

Tristan's heart sank.

When Philip had left, Ivy said, "It's getting late. The others will be here soon. I'd better change."

"I'll help you pick out something," Suzanne said.

"No. Go on down. I'll be with you in a few minutes."

"But you know how I like to pick out clothes for you—"

"We're going," Beth said, pushing Suzanne toward the door. "Take all the time you want, Ivy. If the guys get here, we'll stall." She pulled the door closed behind Suzanne.

Ivy looked across her room at the photograph of Tristan. She stood as still as a statue, tears running down her cheeks.

Lacey said softly, "Tristan, you need to rest now. There's nothing you can do until you rest."

But he could not leave Ivy. He put his arms around her. She slipped through him and moved toward the bureau, taking the picture in her hands. He wrapped her in his arms again, but she only cried harder.

Then Ella was set lightly on the bureau top. Lacey's hands had done it. The cat rubbed up against Ivy's head.

"Oh, Ella. I don't know how to let go of him."

"Don't let go," Tristan begged.

"In the end, she must," Lacey warned.

"I've lost him, Ella, I know it. Tristan is dead. He can't hold me ever again. He can't think of me. He can't want me now. Love ends with death."

"It doesn't!" Tristan said. "I'll hold you again,

I swear it, and you'll see that my love will never end."

"You're exhausted, Tristan," Lacey told him.

"I'll hold you, I'll love you forever!"

"If you don't rest now," Lacey said, "you'll become even more confused. It'll be hard to tell real from unreal, or to rouse yourself out of the darkness. Tristan, listen to me. . . ."

But before she finished speaking, the darkness overtook him.

16

"Well," said Suzanne as the group of them filed out of the movie theater, "in the last few weeks, I think we've seen at least as many films as Siskel and Ebert."

"I'm not sure they went to see that one," Will observed.

"It's the only flick I've liked so far," Eric said. "Can't wait till they do *Bloodbath IV.*"

Gregory glanced over at Ivy. She turned her head.

Ivy was the one who suggested a movie whenever someone told her she needed to get out, which was often lately. If it had been up to her, she'd sit through a triple feature. Occasionally she lost herself in the story, but even if she didn't, it was a way of looking sociable without having to talk. Unfortunately, the easiest part of the evening was over now. Ivy winced when they came out of the cinema's cool, dark otherworld and into the hot, neon-lit night.

"Pizza?" Gregory asked.

"I could use a drink," said Suzanne.

"Well, Gregory's buying, since he wouldn't let me stock the trunk," Eric told her.

"Gregory's buying pizza," Gregory said.

More and more, Ivy thought, Gregory was coming to resemble a camp counselor, shepherding around this odd flock of people, acting responsible. It was a wonder that Eric put up with it—but she knew that Gregory, Will, and Eric still had their own nights out, nights with wilder girls and guys.

On these group dates Ivy played a game with herself, seeing how long she could go without thinking about Tristan, or at least without missing him terribly. She worked at paying attention to those around her. Life went on for them, even if it didn't for her.

That night they headed for Celentano's, a popular pizza parlor. Their chairs wobbled and the tablecloths were squares of torn-off paper—Crayons and Pencils Provided, a sign said—but the owners, Pat and Dennis, were gourmet all the way. Beth, who loved anything with chocolate, adored their famous dessert pizzas.

"What's it going to be tonight?" Gregory teased her. "Brownies and cheese?"

Beth smiled, two pink streaks showing high in her cheeks. Part of Beth's prettiness was her openness, Ivy thought, her way of smiling at you without holding back.

"I'm getting something different. Something healthy. I've got it! Brie with apricots and shavings of bitter chocolate!"

Gregory laughed and laid his hand lightly on Beth's shoulder. Ivy thought back to the time when she had been mystified by some of Gregory's comments and convinced that he could only mock her and her friends.

But now she found him pretty easy to figure out. Like his father, he had a temper and he needed to be appreciated. At the moment, both Beth and Suzanne were appreciating him, Suzanne watching him more shrewdly, glancing over the top of her menu.

"All I want is pepperoni," Eric complained. "Just pepperoni." He was running his finger up and down and across the list of pizzas, up and down and across, like a frustrated mouse that couldn't find its way out of a maze.

Will had apparently made up his mind. His menu was closed and he had begun drawing on the paper tablecloth in front of him.

"Well, Rembrandt returns," said Pat, passing

by their table, nodding toward Will. "Here for lunch three times this week," she explained to the others. "I'd like to think it's our cooking, but I know it's the free art materials."

Will gave her a smile, but it was more with his eyes, which were deep brown, than with his mouth. His lips turned up slightly at just one corner of his mouth.

He was not easy to figure out, thought Ivy.

"O'Leary," said Eric when the owner had passed by, "have you got the hots for Pat, or what?"

"Likes those older women," Gregory teased. "One at UCLA, one doing Europe instead of college . . ."

"You're kidding," said Suzanne, obviously impressed.

Will glanced up. "We're friends," he said, and continued sketching. "And I work next door, at the photo lab."

That was news to Ivy. None of Gregory's friends had real jobs.

"Will did that portrait of Pat," Gregory told the girls.

It was tacked up on the wall, a piece of cheap paper worked over with wax crayons. But it was Pat all right, with her straight, soft hair and hazel eyes and generous mouth—he had found her beauty.

217

"You're really good," said Ivy.

Will's eyes flicked up and held hers for a second, then he continued his drawing. For the life of her she didn't know if he was trying to be cool or if he was just shy.

"You know, Will," said Beth, "Ivy keeps wondering if you're really cool or just shy."

Will blinked.

"Beth!" said Ivy. "Where did that come from?"

"Well, haven't you wondered it? Oh, well, maybe it was Suzanne. Maybe it was me. I don't know, Ivy, my mind's a muddle. I've had a kind of headache since I left your house. I think I need caffeine."

Gregory laughed. "That chocolate pizza should do the job."

"For the record," Will said to Beth, "I'm not really cool."

"Give me a break," Gregory said.

Ivy sat back in her chair and glanced at her watch. Well, it had been eight whole minutes that she had thought about other people. Eight whole minutes without imagining what it would have been like if Tristan had been sitting beside her. That was progress.

Pat took their order. Then she dug in her pocket and handed some forms to Will. "I'm doing this in front of your friends, so you can't

218

back out, Will. I've been saving your tablecloths—I'm planning to sell them once your paintings are hanging in the Metropolitan Museum. But if you don't enter some of your work in the festival, I'm entering the tablecloths."

"Thanks for letting me choose, Pat," he said dryly.

"Do you have any more of those forms?" asked Suzanne. "Ivy needs one."

"You've been saving my tablecloths, too?" Ivy asked.

"Your *music,* girl. The Stonehill Festival is for all kinds of artists. They set up a stage for live performances. This will be good for you."

Ivy bit her tongue. She was so tired of people telling her what would be good for her. Every time somebody said that, all she could think was, Tristan is good for me.

Two minutes this time, two minutes without thinking of him.

Pat brought more festival forms along with their pizzas. The others reminisced about the summer arts festivals of the past.

"I liked watching the dancers," Gregory said.

"I was once a young dancer," Beth told him.

"Till an untimely accident ended her career," Suzanne remarked.

"I was six," Beth said, "and it was all quite magical—flitting around in my sequined costume, a thousand stars sparkling above me. Unfortunately, I danced right off the stage." Will laughed out loud. It was the first time Ivy had heard him laugh like that.

"Do you remember when Richmond played the accordion?"

"Mr. Richmond, our principal?"

Gregory nodded. "The mayor moved a stool out of his way."

"Then Richmond sat down," said Eric.

"Yow!"

Ivy laughed with everyone else, though mostly she was acting. Whenever something did interest her or make her laugh, the first second it held her attention, and the next second she thought, I'll have to tell Tristan.

Four minutes this time.

Will was drawing funny little scenes on the tablecloth: Beth twirling on her toes, Richmond's legs flying upward. He put the scenes together like a comic strip. His hands were quick, his strokes strong and sure. For a few moments, Ivy watched with interest.

Then Suzanne breathed out with a hiss. Ivy glanced sideways, but Suzanne's face was a mask of friendliness. "Here comes a friend of yours," she said to Gregory.

Everyone turned around. Ivy swallowed hard. It was Twinkie Hammonds, the "little, petite" brunette, as Suzanne called her—the girl that Ivy had talked to the day she first saw Tristan swim. And with her was Gary.

Gary was staring at Ivy. Then he checked out Will, who was seated next to her, then Eric and Gregory. Ivy prickled. It wasn't as if she were on a date; still, she felt Gary's eyes accusing her.

"Hi, Ivy."

"Hi."

"Having a good time?" he asked.

She toyed with a crayon, then nodded her head. "Yes."

"Haven't seen you for a while."

"I know," she said, though she had seen him— at the mall once, and another time in town. She had quickly ducked inside the nearest doorway.

"Getting out a lot now?" he asked.

"Pretty much, I guess."

Each time she saw him, she expected Tristan to be nearby.

Each time she had to go through the pain all over again.

"Thought you were. Twinkie told me."

"You got a problem with that?" asked Gregory.

"I was talking to her, not you," Gary replied coolly, "and I was just wondering how she was doing." He shifted his weight from foot to foot. "Tristan's parents were asking about you the other day."

221

Ivy lowered her head.

"I visit them sometimes."

"Good," she said. She had promised herself a hundred times that she would go see them.

"They get lonely," Gary said.

"I guess they do." She made dark little X's with her crayon.

"They like to talk about Tristan."

She nodded silently. She couldn't go to that house again, she couldn't! She laid the crayon down.

"They still have your picture in his room."

Her eyes were dry. But her breath was ragged. She tried to suck it in and let it out evenly, so no one would notice.

"Your picture has a note tucked under it." Gary's voice wavered with a kind of tremulous laughter. "You know the kind of parents they are—were. Always respecting Tristan and his privacy. Even now they won't read it, but they know it's your handwriting and that he saved it. They figure it's some kind of love note and should stay with your picture."

What had she written? Nothing valuable enough to save. Just notes confirming the time they would meet for their next lesson. And he had saved such a scrap.

Ivy fought back the tears. She should never have gone out with the others that night. She couldn't keep her act together long enough.

"You jerk!" It was Gregory's voice.

"It's okay," said Ivy.

"Get out of here, jerk, before I make you!" Gregory ordered.

"It's okay!" She meant it. Gary couldn't help how he felt, any more than she could.

"I told you, Gary," Twinkie said, "she's not the kind to wear black for a year."

Gregory's chair fell back as he rose, and he kicked it away.

Dennis Celentano collared him just before he got to the other side of the table. "What's the trouble here, guys?"

Ivy sat still with her head down. At one time she would have prayed to her angels for strength, but she couldn't anymore. She held herself still, wrapping her arms around herself. She shut down all thoughts, all feelings; she blocked out all the angry words that whirled around her. Numb, she would stay numb; if only she could stay numb forever.

Why hadn't she died instead of him? Why had it happened the way it did? Tristan had been all his parents had. He had been all she wanted. No one could take his place. She should have died, not him!

The room was suddenly quiet, deathly quiet around her. Had she said that out loud? Gary was gone now. She couldn't hear anything but the scratching of a pencil. Will's hand moved quickly, with strokes strong and even more certain than before.

Ivy watched with numb fascination. Finally Will drew back his hand. She stared at the drawings. Angels, angels, angels. One angel that looked like Tristan, his arms wrapped around her lovingly.

Fury rushed through her. "How dare you!" she said. "*How dare you, Will!*"

His eyes met hers. There was confusion and panic in them. But she did not relent. She felt nothing but fury.

"Ivy, I don't know why . . . I didn't mean . . . I'd never want to, Ivy, I swear I never would—"

She ripped the paper off the table.

He stared at it in disbelief. "I'd never hurt you," he said quietly.

It had been so easy. In less than a millisecond, it seemed, Tristan had slipped inside Will. There was no struggling to communicate: the angel pictures had come quickly, as if their minds were one. He had shared Will's amazement at the sight of the image his pencil had drawn; if only Will could make it real for them, his comforting Ivy.

"What do I do now, Lacey?" Tristan asked.

"How can I help Ivy, when all I do is keep hurting her?"

But Lacey wasn't around to give advice.

Tristan wandered the streets of the silent town long after Ivy and her companions had left. He needed to think things out. He was almost afraid to try again. Statues of angels, pictures of angels, just mentioning angels stirred up in Ivy nothing but pain and anger—but that's what he was now, her angel.

His new powers were useless, completely useless. And there was still the question of his mission, about which he was totally ignorant. It was so hard to think about that, when all he could think about was reaching Ivy.

"What do I do now, Lacey?" he asked again.

He wondered if Lacey was being overly dramatic when she had said that his mission could be to save somebody from disaster. But what if she was right? And what if he was so caught up in his and Ivy's pain that he failed someone?

Lacey had said to stay close to the people he knew, which was why, as soon as he awakened from the darkness, he'd sought out Gary and followed him to Celentano's that evening. She'd also told him that the clue to his mission might be in the past, some problem he saw but did not recognize as such. He needed to figure out how to travel back in time.

He imagined time as a whirling net that held thoughts and feelings and actions together, a net that had held him until he suddenly broke away. It seemed that the easiest point of entry would be his point of exit. Would it help to go to the place itself?

He quickly made his way along the dark, winding back roads. It was quite late now and no cars were on the road. An eerie kind of feeling, the sense that at any moment a deer might leap out in front of him, made him slow down, but only for a moment.

It was strange how easily he found the spot and how certain he was that it *was* the spot, for each turn and twist in the road looked the same. The moon, though it was full, barely filtered through the heavy leaves. There was no silver splash of light here, just a lightening of the air, a kind of ghostly gray mist. Still, he found the roses.

Not the ones he had given her, but roses like them. They lay on the side of the road, completely wilted. When he picked them up, their petals fell off like charred flakes; only their purple satin ribbon had survived.

Tristan looked down the road as if he could look back into time. He tried to remember the last minute of being alive. The light. An incredible light and voice, or message—he wasn't sure if it was actually a voice and couldn't remember any words. But that had come after the explosion of light. He returned to the light again and focused his mind on it.

A pinpoint of light—yes, before the tunnel, before the dazzling light at the end, there had been a pinpoint of light, the light in the deer's eye.

Tristan shuddered. He braced himself. Then his whole self felt the impact. He felt as if he were collapsing in on himself. He fell back. The car was rushing backward, like an amusement park ride suddenly thrown in reverse. He was caught in a tape running backward, with words of gibberish and frantic motions. He tried to stop it, willed it to stop, every bit of his energy bent on stopping the backward-racing time.

Then he and Ivy sat side by side, absolutely still, as if frozen in a movie frame. They were in the car and eased slowly forward now.

"Last glimpse of the river," he said as the road made a sharp turn away from it.

The June sun, dropping over the west ridge of the Connecticut countryside, shafted light on the very tops of the trees, flaking them with gold. The winding road slipped below, into a tunnel of maples, poplars, and oaks. It was like slipping under dark green waves. Tristan flicked on his headlights.

"You really don't have to hurry," said Ivy. "I'm not hungry anymore."

"I ruined your appetite?"

She shook her head. "I guess I'm all filled up with happiness," she said softly.

The car sped along and took a curve sharply.

"I said, we don't have to hurry."

"That's funny," he murmured. "I wonder what's—" He glanced down at his feet. "This doesn't feel . . ."

"Slow down, okay? It doesn't matter if we're a little late— Oh!" Ivy pointed straight ahead. "Tristan!"

Something had plunged through the bushes and into the roadway. He saw it, too, a flicker of motion among the deep shadows. Then the deer stopped. It turned its head, its eyes drawn to the car's bright headlights.

"Tristan!" she shouted.

He braked harder. They were rushing toward the shining eyes.

"Tristan, don't you see it?"

"Ivy, something's—"

"A deer!"

He braked again and again, the pedal pressed flat to the floor, but the car wouldn't slow down.

The animal's eyes blazed. Then light came from behind it, a burst of headlights—a car was coming from the opposite direction. Trees walled them in. There was no room to steer to the left or the right, and the brake pedal was flat against the floor.

"Stop!" she shouted.

"I'm—"

"Stop, why don't you stop?" she pleaded. "Tristan, *stop!*"

He willed the car to stop, he willed himself back into the present, but he had no control, nothing would stop him from speeding into the whirling funnel of darkness. It swallowed him up.

When he opened his eyes, Lacey was peering down at him.

"Rough ride?"

Tristan looked around. He was still on the wooded road, but it was early morning now, gold light fragile as spiderwebs netting the trees. He tried to remember what had happened.

"You called me, hours ago, asked me what to do next," she reminded him. "Obviously you couldn't wait to find out."

"I went back," he said, and then in a rush he remembered. "Lacey, it wasn't just the deer. If it hadn't been the deer, it would have been a wall. Or trees or the river or the bridge. It could have been another car."

229

"Slow down, Tristan! What are you saying?"

"There was no pressure, no fluid. It went all the way down to the floor."

"What did?" Lacey asked.

"The pedal. The brake. It shouldn't have given out like that." He grabbed Lacey. "What if . . . what if it wasn't an accident? What if it only looked like one?"

"And you only look dead," she replied. "Sure fooled me."

"Listen to me, Lacey. Those brakes were in perfect shape. Somebody must have messed with them. Somebody cut the line! You have to help me."

"But I don't even know how to pump gas," she said.

"You have to help me reach Ivy!" Tristan started down the road.

"I'd rather work on the brakes," Lacey called after him. "Slow down, Tristan. Before you knock off another deer."

But nothing would stop him. "Ivy has to believe again," Tristan said. "We have to reach her. She has to know that it wasn't an accident. Somebody wanted me—or Ivy—dead!"

Don't miss the thrilling continuation of

KISSED BY AN ANGEL

Volume II:
The Power of Love

Ivy's flesh turned to goose bumps, but she fought back against her fear. She crept down the steps and stopped just inside the door that led to the hall. She wished Ella was with her; the cat could warn her of any real danger with a prick of her ears or a jerk of her tail.

"Ella?" Ivy called.

No answer.

"Ella, come here. Where are you, Ella?"

The house was silent.

Ivy tiptoed into the hall toward down the center stair. There was a phone on the table in the lower hall. If she noticed that anything had been disturbed, she'd immediately make a call from there.

Ivy walked through the dining room, tensing

at the creak of old boards, and pushed open the door to the kitchen. Across from her was the door she had left unlocked earlier, still closed.

Just as she locked it, Ella came trotting toward her.

"Ella!" Ivy breathed out with relief. "What have you been up to? Where have you—"

Before Ivy could finish a bag was pulled over her head. She screamed and fought to get free, ripping at the bag with her hands. The more she yanked at the bag, though, the tighter it was pulled around her. She was suffocating.

She began to kick and kick, and shriek.

Then she heard a pounding sound from somewhere else in the house. Someone was pounding and calling "Ivy! Ivy!"

She tried to answer.

Suddenly, she was hurtled forward and could not stop herself from falling. She slammed against something hard as rock and slid down it. Metal things tumbled and clattered around her. Then everything went black.

About the Author

Elizabeth Chandler has written picture books, chapter books, middle grade novels, and young adult romances under a variety of names. Her guardian angel knows her as Mary Claire Helldorfer (but keep that a secret, please). She lives in Baltimore, and loves stories, cats, baseball, and Bob—not necessarily in that order.